TIME OF THE DEMON

or

INCIDENT AT THE HALF MOON INN

by

Ian Taylor and Rosi Taylor

A Story Based on Actual Events

Copyright (C) 2019 Ian Taylor and Rosi Taylor

Layout design and Copyright (C) 2019 by Next Chapter

Published 2021 by Next Chapter

Edited by Tyler Colins

Cover art by Cover Mint

Back cover texture by David M. Schrader, used under license from Shutterstock.com

Mass Market Paperback Edition

This book is a work of fiction. Names, characters, places, and incidents are the product of the authors imaginations or have been used fictitiously. Any resemblance to actual events, locales, or persons, living or dead, is purely coincidental.

All rights reserved. No part of this book may be reproduced or transmitted in any form or by any means, electronic or mechanical, including photocopying, recording, or by any information storage and retrieval system, without the authors' permissions.

1

It was 5.30 p.m. on a weekday evening in early November. The weather was dry with a low cloud ceiling of sombre and oppressive cumulus. The rush hour traffic was heavy on the main road that lay between two major English cities. Although it was not yet completely dark, the road was a ribbon of headlights.

A double-decker bus pulled in at a bus stop on the main road. Two twenty-something barmaids, Jessica Bryce and Georgina Lovell (not their real names), got off the bus and headed towards the nearby Half Moon Inn, that stood back from the road behind a fenced-off forecourt of low-maintenance shrubs.

The inn and its original ranges of stables and outbuildings had undergone a series of transformations during its two-hundred-year history. For the first half of its life it had been a wayside hostelry, which had closed with the advent of motor transport. Its buildings had become a seed corn and potato merchant's premises, and then a stud. The whole complex had lain derelict during the war years, then been bulldozed away in the 1950s to make room for a purpose-built pub, which bore the same name as the original hostelry. The current building was leased from a local landowner by a national pub chain.

On this particular evening the place lay in darkness, as the inn did not officially open till 6:00 p.m. Jess and Gina walked around to what was now the main entrance off the customers' car park at the rear of the building. They had to use their torches, as there were no lights in the vicinity, the car park backing on to open pastureland that was divided into small fields by eighteenth-century enclosure hedges.

"No Graham–again," Jess commented peevishly, stepping around the puddles from the afternoon's rain showers.

"He gets paid for doing nothing," Gina added sourly. "Some people just chance their luck and get away with it! We're not paid to be acting managers."

"It's not fair," Jess agreed. "It shouldn't be our responsibility to open up."

"Complain," Gina suggested. "You've been here longer than me, so it should come from you."

"I might."

"You won't. You never do."

"I *might*. It's just that Graham knows the area boss really well. I could end up losing my job. I'd need a reference from him if I left and he knows it."

It was almost dark at the back of the inn. In what little daylight remained the girls could see that the car park was empty of vehicles. Beyond the boundary fence nothing could be discerned of the open countryside. As Jess fumbled in her handbag for the keys to the main door, Gina became aware of a bright white light that suddenly appeared beneath the low cloud above the fields behind the car park. She nudged her companion's arm.

"What's that?"

The girls watched the light for a few seconds. It seemed to be moving slowly and it made no sound.

"It's just a plane," Jess said. Then, less certainly, "isn't it?"

Gina was puzzled. "I can't hear engines. It can't be a plane!"

"Maybe it's one of those gliders from the club on the airfield."

Gina was doubtful. "Who'd be out gliding in the dark? And it's getting lower."

"It's not going to clear those trees!" Jess stared in sudden horror at the approaching light.

"Oh my God," Gina shrieked. "Did you see that? It went straight through them—straight through those trees!"

The light seemed to pass through a stand of mature pines and then land in the field beyond the car park. But it didn't go out. It remained constant, at ground level, very bright and silent.

There was no explosion. No flames. No cries for help.

"It's crashed!" Gina shrieked.

"Better see if we can do something," Jess proposed anxiously.

The girls ran across the car park and climbed the perimeter post-and-rail fence, observing that the light remained constant in the field. On the other side of the fence, they found themselves struggling to make headway against an impenetrable tangle of thorn bushes and briars.

"Ouch! I can't get through," Gina cried out.

The twosome were forced to give up their attempt to reach the field from the car park.

"Let's phone emergency from the office," Jess suggested.

They retreated to the fence, then hurried across the car park towards the inn. Their entire experience, they estimated later, had taken only five or six minutes. As they entered the inn they looked back, noting that the light remained very bright, stationary, and strangely silent.

When questioned the next day by a reporter from the *Evening Courier*, Jess mentioned she'd thought she'd seen something else as she'd looked back from the doorway: the vague impression of a tall figure covered in feathers like some kind of birdman, standing by the fence at the edge of the car park. But then Gina had switched on the outside lights and by the time Jess's eyes had adjusted to the sudden glare, the figure—if it had indeed been there—had vanished.

Time of the Demon

The bar stood in semi-darkness, illuminated by passing traffic on the main road. Jess and Gina flicked on ground-floor lights from the main switchboard. Then, they rushed into the office and Gina grabbed the telephone. By now, both were beginning to panic.

"Shall I dial 999?" Gina asked.

"What else? And be quick!"

Gina hesitated. "Never done this before." She thrust the receiver at Jess. "Here–you do it."

Jess took the phone. "Go out and watch."

Gina ran out as Jess nervously dialled the emergency number.

Standing on the bottom rail of the car park fence, Gina watched the light in the field, shielding her eyes from its brightness. A couple minutes later, Jess was at her side.

"I've rung them," Jess said breathlessly. "I said it was a plane crash and we needed everyone."

"But is it a plane?" Gina asked, confused. "I've been watching, and it's stayed very quiet. No sign of flames. No one's tried to get out and run away. Nothing's happened. There's just the light."

Jess climbed onto the fence next to Gina. They stared at the intense light, protecting their eyes.

"It's very weird." Jess' voice was tinged with awe. "It's not doing anything."

"It's just a light." Gina sounded scared. "There's no shape to it. No bodywork. No wings or anything."

"Hello?" Jess called anxiously. "Is anyone there?"

Silence.

"Is anyone hurt?" Gina shouted uncertainly. "Do you need help?"

Silence.

The girls looked at each other with escalating confusion and fear. Their mounting anxiety was interrupted by the sound of rapidly approaching sirens from the main road.

I don't believe it—they're here already," Jess exclaimed. "I've only just rung them!"

Three vehicles appeared, blue lights flashing. All were police cars; there was no sign of fire engines or ambulances. They swooped past the car park, heading down the rough track that led to the field beyond the fence.

"We'd better tell them what we saw," Jess said decisively.

Gina looked doubtful. "You do the talking. I don't like officials."

"We should go back into the bar. We *are* supposed to be at work," Jess reasoned. "They'll find us if they want us."

* * *

A helicopter appeared and hovered above the flashing police cars, the power of its searchlight muting the white glow of the light in the field.

Although a number of personnel were in attendance at the scene, none of them had yet entered the field. The officers seemed content merely to observe from the comfort of their vehicles. This would, incidentally, prove an important point researchers recalled later.

Janet (Jan) Barnes, a thirty-year-old reporter from the *Evening Courier*, drove into the car park in a 4x4 BMW. She pulled up, opened her window and peered out, then made a call on her mobile.

"Hi Russell. I'm out at the Half Moon Inn and it looks like some kind of incident. ...No, I don't know yet. Blue lights flashing and there's a chopper with its searchlight on. I can't see any other press, so I must be the first here. Could be our lucky night–a scoop for the *Courier*!"

She rang off and got out of her car. As she walked on to the rough track, she noted a dark-coloured Mercedes pull into the car park behind her. Two men dressed in well-cut suits got out and entered the inn. Her reporter's instinct told her they weren't paying customers, more like officials of some kind. Her brain all at once began yelling, *"Story, story, story!"*

Should she approach the officers in the cars, or find out what the suits were up to? She decided on the latter.

Halfway back across the car park, she was intercepted by a uniformed officer. Where the hell had he sprung from? The man was very tall and lean, and had a clipped affected voice that could have come from a broadcast of *British Pathé News*. Weren't such affectations obsolete now, she wondered later.

"Superintendent Hemingway," he announced. "I'm the officer in charge here. Can I help you?"

She knew everyone on the local force and they didn't have a Hemingway, which struck her as odd. She showed him her press ID. "Jan Barnes, *Evening Courier*. I'm enquiring about the incident in the field back there." She watched the man's body language closely. Sometimes, even among professionals, it gave away more than their words. But, annoyingly, Hemingway's didn't.

"I'm afraid I can't comment," the officer clipped. "I must ask you to leave immediately while we make sure the area is secure. Your personal safety could be at risk."

"Is it a crime scene?" she asked, undaunted. "A terrorist incident?"

"I'm afraid I can't go into details."

"Well, something's happened–or you wouldn't be here!"

She sensed the superintendent's manner soften. Ah, she thought, he's going to give me the official line.

"All I can tell you is that two young people thought they saw an aircraft crash in the field back there," Hemingway began. "However, it seems they were mistaken. They're not trained observers, after all."

"So what *did* they see?" she persisted.

Hemingway stiffened. "I must consult with my colleagues before I can give you the definitive answer to that. But, as of this moment, we've found nothing."

"So these witnesses didn't see *anything*?" she continued. "But my personal safety might still be at risk? I'd call that a contradiction, wouldn't you?" She had him—and Hemingway knew it.

He cleared his throat, gaining time to collect himself. "It appears the witnesses may, errr ... may have overreacted to what were most likely the reflections of aeroplane lights on a low cloud ceiling. That's our thinking at the moment. But when there's a chance that life could be in danger, every emergency call has to be taken with the utmost seriousness."

Blah, blah, blah, she thought. "It's just a false alarm then?" She watched the superintendent closely.

"It seems so, yes," Hemingway replied. Then, with the hint of a reassuring smile, added, "But it was a call of good intent."

"So if nothing's happened, what's with the light back there?" she asked. "I can see a light in the field. You don't have to be a trained observer to see that!"

He suppressed his rising anger. He's lying, she thought. What was he trying to hide?

"It's the helicopter's searchlight reflecting off the ground surface," the superintendent stated. "I assure you, it's nothing more. Please leave now—and have a safe and pleasant evening, Ms Barnes."

He walked away. She was about to chase after him when she spotted a handsome dark-haired stranger in his mid-thirties talking with another officer near the car park entrance. Slow to shift her curious gaze, they made eye contact. She was taken aback by the intensity of his stare.

"My, you've got a look," she said to herself as she hurried to the inn entrance, where she found a large uniformed officer blocking her way. She flashed her press ID and attempted to breeze past. "Jan Barnes, *Evening Courier*. I'd just like a quick word with the staff."

The officer, stolid and unyielding, continued to block the entrance. "No one's allowed in. No questions. No cameras. Just leave."

She stood her ground. "It must be a serious incident then." She looked him straight in the eye. "Has anyone been injured?"

He returned her penetrating gaze without blinking. The irrational notion came to her that he could be a robot.

"I'm not able to comment," the robot replied. "Please leave."

She noticed that the officer's uniform bore no identifying insignia, no rank or number. Come to think of it, she realised with a shock, neither had Hemingway's. Her suspicions deepened. "Which force are you with?" she asked. "Are you from outside the county?"

"I'm sorry," the officer replied, staring at her impassively, "I'm not able to answer any of your questions."

Thwarted, she went back to her 4x4 and drove away. She noted, with an unexpected twinge of disappointment, that the dark-haired stranger had gone.

But there was a story behind the rebuttals, no doubt of it–and it was damn well going to be hers!

She pulled into a lay-by on a quiet country lane, got out and scanned the crash site with her night glasses. She was on slightly higher ground and could clearly see the helicopter hovering above the field, its searchlight illuminating the area. But the bright white light she'd noticed earlier had disappeared.

The blue lights of the police vehicles still flashed, but there were no officers anywhere in the field.

Had they found something? If so, it must have been small enough to fit into the back of a car. Was it debris from some secret weapon? She suddenly felt very cold when she realised how little she knew of her country's covert military activities.

As she turned to get back in her car, she had the fleeting impression of huge feathery wings passing overhead. An owl? No, owls weren't that big. A heron? But herons weren't nocturnal, were they? She dismissed the mystery, got in the car and rang the local air-traffic control.

"It's Jan Barnes at the *Evening Courier*. I just wondered if you'd had anything unusual on your screens tonight? ... Nothing on SSR? No missing aircraft or anything weird? ...Nothing? ...Is that official? ...Okay. Many thanks."

Annoyed and mystified, she rang off and drove away.

* * *

She went straight back to her flat in the city, to the west of the Half Moon Inn, and flopped onto the sofa, skimming TV news channels. Fragments of news stories filled her room: the proxy war rumbled on in Yemen, ISIS claimed responsibility for a bomb attack on a Kabul wedding party, the bodies of more African refugees had been washed up in the Med....

What a mess we've made of the planet, she thought for the thousandth time. But there was no mention of a plane crash in the north of England.

She glared at the screen in vexation, leaped up and paced the room, talking on her mobile to a contact at the local hospital.

"And no one's been brought in? No accident victims at all? ...We're talking about the same thing here, out at the Half Moon Inn? ...Okay. Sorry to bother you. Thanks."

Was it a military drone that had come down in the field? It seemed the most likely answer. If it was, what might it have been carrying to produce such a light?

She went to her desk, switched on her laptop and made a Skype call. The weary face of her editor, fifty-five-year-old Russell Furlong, appeared on the screen. She knew he was working at home; she could see study bookshelves behind him. Poor old Russell, she thought. The paper's owners never let him rest.

"Hi Russell. What's with the plane crash?" she asked, hoping he had an answer.

Russell pulled a face. "No idea. You tell me."

Time of the Demon

"I got a tip-off from a fire guy I know. One of my best contacts. It sounded bona fide. I spoke to a Superintendent Hemingway at the scene. He made out it was a false alarm. Do you know this guy?"

Russell shook his head. "Nope, sorry. Never heard of a Hemingway."

"I thought he was very high rank for a non-event." She didn't mention the absence of insignia.

Russell nodded. "I agree with you."

"And there were only police cars there. No fire service or paramedics. But, oddly, they had a chopper with a huge searchlight. Why scramble that if they thought it was a non-event?"

"Nothing on national or local news?" Russell asked with a furrowed brow.

"Zero. I did local radio coming back in the car and the TV news just now."

"What does your reporter's nose tell you?"

"That it's definitely off."

"Follow it for now," he advised. "But tread carefully with the police."

He disconnected. She stared thoughtfully at the empty screen. Then she rang the fireman who had given her the original tip-off.

"Hi Baz, it's Jan from the *Courier*. What happened to the crashed plane? ...You were almost at the scene and then stood down? ...And the paramedics too? ...For God's sake why? ...A misidentification? ...Oh, shit, too bad." She decided it was time to lie. "No, I was sent after a different story, so I never got there at all. That's why I'm ringing you. Bit of good luck for me as it turned out, eh? ...Same to you. Keep in touch."

Over the years her reporter's instinct for a good story had served her well and right now it was telling her that this could be a big one and, with the aid of a timely lie, she'd made it all her own. How big the story would actually become she couldn't possibly have guessed.

2

News items crammed the bulletin board in the Transatlantic UFO Networks (TRUFON) local office. Gregory Houseman, the thirty-five-year-old good-looking stranger Jan had spotted in the Half Moon car park, studied them carefully.

Dan and Jake, two young UFO buffs, sat at a large table strewn with genre magazines and empty polystyrene coffee cups, hard at work on their laptops. Gregory turned to them.

"It's all old news on here. Thought there was a flap?"

Dan looked up. "According to a highly-placed source, we're supposed to be experiencing a surge of UFO-related activity." He raised his fingers as inverted commas. "The cops are on red alert, which means they're doing nothing."

"So if you've got everything from LITS to CE4s, it's all too hush-hush to put up on the board," Gregory smiled at his implied jest.

"I wish!" Jake laughed. "Nothing's happening. Some school kids said they saw Owlman in a car park in town. That's about it."

"*The* Owlman?" Gregory asked wryly.

Dan shrugged. "Who knows? Scared 'em half to death."

"But otherwise, it's quiet," Jake admitted. "Till last night."

"I got wind of something out at the Half Moon," Gregory advised. "But I wasn't able to get there."

"The official line is it was some kind of misidentification." Dan pulled a sceptical face.

Jake shrugged. "We're stumped. No one in the world of 'officialdom' is saying *anything*."

"What's your gut instinct tell you?" Gregory persisted, watching both men for any hint of hostility. If they became suspicious of him—and suspicion was every UFO researcher's predominant emotion—he'd have to back off.

"We're being shut out," Dan said irritably.

"Ergo, it could be big," Jake added, nodding sagaciously.

Gregory stepped towards the door. "I'll do some digging. Get back to you."

"Who is that guy?" Dan asked when Gregory had gone.

Jake shrugged. "I've seen him around. He said he's a friend of Neil's."

"*Which* Neil?" Dan asked with a frown.

* * *

Next morning Jan headed east along the main road. She passed the inn and noticed its frontage had been surrounded with official police tape. She pulled into an American-style diner, which was situated a hundred yards further along the road, on the opposite side. The diner's car park had a good view of the inn and the field behind it. She got out and scanned the area to the rear of the inn through binoculars.

A large sign blocking the inn's car park entrance read: POLICE NOTICE NO ADMITTANCE. Three figures in full protective gear plodded around in the adjacent field. There didn't seem to be any wreckage–if there'd been any, it must have been removed. The figures appeared to be concerned with taking soil and plant samples.

A man in a trim city suit appeared at the car park entrance and began surveying the surrounding area through field glasses. All at once he aimed the glasses at Jan. She whipped her binoculars out of sight and turned quickly, hoping her reaction had been fast enough not to arouse suspicion. "What the hell is this?" she muttered.

She entered the diner and took a window seat overlooking the main road. The place wasn't busy, with no more than a dozen customers scattered among the tables. She ordered a burger and coffee, and stared from the window at the taped-off inn until the waitress returned and served her.

"What's happened there?" Jan asked innocently. "Is it some kind of crime scene?"

"No idea." The middle-aged waitress glanced indifferently in the direction of the inn. "It was like that when I got here this morning."

"The inn's only open in the evenings, isn't it?" Jan asked casually.

"They open at six. There's supposed to be a manager, but he's never there."

"So who does the work?"

"Couple of girls run the bar, Jess and Gina. They do sandwiches and snacks. Pretty good stuff, actually. Sometimes, if we're open, they come in to get change."

Jan was pleased to find that the waitress was happy to talk. She wanted to find these two girls and saw her chance.

"They local?" she asked.

The waitress named a suburb of the city to the east. "They told me they live in that block of 'sixties' flats by the river."

Jan sipped coffee and smiled amiably. "You make a really mean coffee."

The waitress seemed pleased with the compliment. "Thanks."

Jan felt she had made a positive contact. "Were you working last night?"

The woman shook her head. "We shut at five-thirty November to February."

With a quick smile and nod, she left Jan to her burger. Her information ruled the diner out for potential witnesses. That only left the two girls, the *untrained observers*.

As Jan headed for her BMW, she spotted Gregory Houseman sitting at the wheel of an Audi Estate, studying what looked like a road map. She stared at him, but he did not return her gaze. Reaching her car, she glanced back and caught him watching. She scowled. "Get a *good* look, why don't you?" she asked quietly.

* * *

After a couple of false starts Jan found the girls' flat and rang the bell. There was no response. She tried again. The door opened an inch and Jess peered through the crack.

Jan produced her press ID. "Hi. I'm from–"

"What do you want?" The tone was seriously hostile.

Jan pocketed her press card and changed tack. "I'm trying to locate the manager of the Half Moon Inn. I understand you work there."

Jess appeared relieved and opened the door a little wider. She was dressed in an old fleecy robe and looked as if she hadn't slept a wink all night. Her eyes were red and looked extremely sore. The remains of her eye make-up were smeared across her cheeks. Jan wondered if she had been crying. But it would have required a prolonged period of distress to leave eyes as inflamed as that.

Jess frowned. "You want Graham Turner?"

"I do. Perhaps you have his address? Or phone number?"

"It's a mobile number. I can never remember it." Jess sounded exhausted. She opened the door fully. "You'd better come in."

Jan found herself in the living room, which was a typical example of 'sixties' plain functionality. The room was untidy. The furniture was cheap and had seen better days. The thin carpet was worn and stained. Lower-end furnished flat, she thought. A five-fifty a month buy-to-let.

Memorabilia and framed photos from Mediterranean holidays stood on shelves and the windowsill. Some of them showed Jess and Gina in the company of a variety of young men, obviously Spaniards or Italians. Jan surreptitiously slipped a photo of the girls into her handbag.

Gina, in a threadbare robe, sat on the sofa. In front of her, on the coffee table, were unwashed mugs and opened packets of biscuits. Gina also looked as if she hadn't slept and her eyes seemed more inflamed than Jess'.

"I'm Jess and this is Gina. This lady wants Graham's mobile number." The hostility had gone from Jess's voice, and conveyed a combination of confusion and anxiety she made no attempt to hide.

Gina got reluctantly to her feet and went to a cupboard drawer. "I put it in here somewhere."

Time of the Demon

"Actually," Jan hesitated, then plunged on. "It's you two I want to talk to."

"What the hell for?" Jess was instantly suspicious. The hostility in her voice had returned.

Jan produced her press ID. "I'm Jan Barnes from the *Courier*. I wanted to talk about last night."

Both girls became angry and defensive to cover what Jan perceived as fear.

"We've told them all we know," Jess said in furious despair. "Why don't you just leave us alone?"

"We've nothing else to say," Gina put in bluntly.

"They told us not to speak to anyone," Jess added, looking worried.

"Who told you?" Jan asked, trying to sound as empathic as possible.

Jess shrugged. "These guys."

"What guys?" Jan probed.

"The guys in the sharp suits." Gina sounded increasingly uneasy.

"They made threats. They frightened us."

It was obvious to Jan that Jess wasn't lying. Her voice was husky with fear. "Why on earth would they do that?"

Both girls seemed on the brink of tears.

"We were only trying to help," Gina wailed. "We thought someone might have been hurt."

"Just wish we hadn't damn well bothered," Jess complained under her breath.

Jan knew it was crucial to win the girls' confidence. But, if she was too insensitive, they might clam up altogether. "Well you've nothing to fear from me," she began, watching them closely. She felt like a trainer with a pair of skittish racehorses. "I'll do my best to help you. Just take your time and tell me what happened."

"We said we wouldn't," Jess objected. "We've been up all night worrying about it."

"It's not fair," Gina said angrily. "It's like we did something wrong. We'd just arrived at work and we saw this light come down in the field behind the inn. We thought it was a plane." She paused, confused. "Well, what else could it be? And Jess dialled 999."

"And this is where it got us," Jess said bitterly.

Jan made shorthand notes. "And it wasn't a plane or a drone?"

"I don't know," Gina said, sounding increasingly upset. "It was just this very bright white light that came down real slow. But what was weird was there was no sound. No explosion when it hit the ground. The light just seemed to spread out a bit. But it was all silent. Really creepy."

"You told the police all this?" Jan asked with a disarming smile.

Jess took up the story. "We tried. But the police gave us to the guys in the sharp suits. The police said that the inn was closed. Then the suits took us into a back room and we told them what we'd seen."

Gina looked scared. "They got very serious when we told them. They said we shouldn't tell anyone or we'd be in deep trouble. They said it was of national importance—and we should never speak of it again."

"But we've got to talk to someone." Jess seemed genuinely offended. "We feel so alone with this. And that's not right."

"You won't put our names in the paper or anything like that, will you?" Gina looked at Jan, her face filled with alarm.

Jan felt sorry for the girls. It was indeed a frightening predicament. But she wanted the story. It would be obvious to the authorities who'd given her the information. After all, they were the only two witnesses. But the public had a right to know that an unexplained incident had occurred. She heard herself make a promise. "I give you my word that I won't mention you by name. I'll protect your identities."

The girls seemed reassured. Jan sensed new emotions surfacing through their fear.

"I've never been involved in anything like it." Jess's eyes opened wide with bloodshot recollection. "It was like a terrorist attack you see on TV. You know, blue lights and a helicopter and police."

"And they got there so fast," Gina put in, "as if they knew it had happened before we phoned them."

"So what are you saying?" Jan asked.

Jess gave a long puzzled look. "It just seems incredible, but it was like they were *expecting* it."

* * *

As Jan left and made for the car parked a couple of hundred yards away, she spotted Gregory Houseman watching from his Audi Estate. He drove away quickly, but she jumped in her car and pursued. She caught him up five minutes later on a link road to the city's bypass. Pulling level with the Audi, she indicated left and sounded the horn. He acknowledged her with a hoot and a wave, and pulled into a lay-by. She parked in front.

They got out and stared at each other. He smiled amiably. She frowned.

"Impressive. Where did you learn to drive like that?"

He was still smiling, either because his admiration was sincere, or because he was a patronising male chauvinist ... she opted for the latter.

"Who are you?" she asked beligerently. "You're not a cop. I've a nose for cops and you don't smell like one."

"Gregory Houseman, paranormal investigator. And you're Janet Barnes, roving reporter aka lead feature writer for the *Evening Courier*."

He stuck out a muscular hand. She ignored it. "You're a what?"

"I get involved in situations like this."

"Do you now? And what kind of situation d'you think we're in?"

Time of the Demon

"Quite an odd one. There's a lot here that doesn't add up."

She distrusted his overfamiliar manner. He reminded her of a bogus home-insulation salesman, or a door-to-door religious nut—*con man* was stamped on his forehead. She had no idea what a paranormal investigator was, but whatever it was, she didn't want one anywhere near her story.

"If you were waiting to talk to those two girls, you're wasting your time. They won't speak to anyone."

He laughed. "So you spent thirty-six minutes *not* talking about anything? They must have had a lot they *didn't* want to tell you."

She was stunned. He had effortlessly outwitted her and—judging by that widening grin—thought of her as little better than an inept amateur.

"Don't care for the press very much," he said. "I mean the press in general. They nearly always get the facts wrong. Of course," the infuriating smile was there again, "there are always exceptions."

She glared. "I don't get the facts wrong, *Mister* Houseman!"

"Okay, I'm happy to concede that you're one of the few. And it's Greg, please."

"Why are you mocking me?" she replied angrily. "For all you know I might be far better at my job than you are at yours! You could be a patronising failure."

He laughed again. "I'm sure I am—at least some of the time. But I think we should talk. Compare thoughts. I think what happened last night is far bigger than egos and reputations."

In spite of her initial dislike, she couldn't deny she was intrigued by him. It was time to eat a tiny morsel of humble pie. "If you want to talk, you can buy me a coffee," she said, still without smiling.

They got back in their cars and drove off, the BMW leading the way and heading for the bypass. Hidden in a nearby clump of densely-branched bushes, a hideous owl-like figure stared after them.

* * *

Jan and Greg sat with coffees in the American diner, occupying a window table with a clear view of the inn and the field to the rear. The men in protective gear had gone, but the field glasses of a watcher in a first-floor inn window caught the early morning light. Jan and Greg both noticed.

"I wasn't following you," he said, "I was waiting to see who would be calling on those girls. Then you turned up."

"I didn't get to speak to them at the incident last night," she explained with a shrug.

"Neither did I. It was one of those situations where I thought it was far too risky to stick my head above the parapet. I didn't fancy a *tête-à-tête* with the kind of guys who turned up last night." He studied her a moment, his expression growing serious. "You do realise those girls will be under surveillance? Hidden camera in the stairwell most likely. That's why I didn't go in.

You'll be on record now. They'll know your shoe size. Your favourite takeaway. The lot."

She was too surprised to check her sudden outburst. "You're joking! Who the hell's watching them?" Too late she realised she'd exposed her colossal ignorance.

"Probably a unit of Special Branch. They get involved in things like this. There could have been military intelligence guys there too, most likely out of sight in the chopper."

Okay, she thought, time to eat dirt. "What sort of thing *is* this?"

"Not sure yet," he said with a self-deprecating smile. "But my information so far suggests it could be a pretty heavy situation."

"They were out in that field earlier, but there doesn't seem to be any wreckage. It looked like they were taking samples of plants and soil."

"They usually do. Any major UFO event attracts this kind of official attention."

She stared at him, stunned. "What? A UFO?"

"Well, it's too early for Santa Claus and his reindeer!"

She felt inadequate. "I don't know anything about UFOs. I don't know how you think I can be of any help to you."

"I'm not saying it was a UFO. But whatever it was, it's attracted serious official attention. And this is your patch. You know people here. You've got some clout. That could help us a lot." He offered a grin. "In exchange, I'll tell you what I know about the weird world of UFOs." He thrust out a hand. "A deal?"

She studied him. She was distrustful of grins. All too often they disguised secret and sometimes very dodgy agendas. "I might need to go public."

He withdrew his hand. "Best wait till you know a bit more, don't you think?"

She didn't like to put herself at the mercy of this Gregory guy. He'd undoubtedly dump her as soon as he'd used up her helpful contacts. "How much more do I need to know?"

He looked at her for a long moment. "We're only seeing the tip of the iceberg. If it wasn't a UFO, it's something even more sinister."

"Are UFOs sinister?"

"That's a big question. But the short answer is yes, I think they are."

"How do I know I can trust you, or believe a word you say?"

"You don't. But you could get a scoop. And I can help. Is there a deal?" His grin had vanished and he appeared grave, even a little anxious.

"Okay. I'll give it twenty-four hours."

She was going into this with all her doubts before her. But she was intrigued. She watched him relax and sensed his energy rising, focusing. Observing his watchful alertness, she thought of him as a hunter. But all hunters were predators. And some were dangerous.

"Make it thirty-six," he said, easing back in his seat and studying her with dark shrewd eyes. "Midnight tomorrow. After that, if we've made no progress, you can do what you want."

He extended his hand. With the slightest of hesitations, she grasped it.

3

Jan sat at her small cluttered desk in the *Evening Courier's* back office, talking on her office phone. She'd decided to have one more go at chasing Hemingway and began by approaching county forces, starting with the local one and working outwards. Her one-sided conversations went something like this:

"Jan Barnes, yes. B-A-R-N-E-S. Could I speak to Superintendent Hemingway please? ...I'm sorry? ...You've no one with that name? ...But you must. I spoke to him yesterday ...I don't get names wrong. It was Hemingway: H-E-M-I-N-G-W-A-Y. It's not a name you'd easily forget. ...Okay. Suit yourself."

No matter how persistent she was, she got nowhere. After ringing ten county forces, all with negative results, she gave up. She tried the Met, but was put through to someone called Smythe at Personnel, who answered her questions with ones of his own; she found she was on the receiving end of an unlooked-for grilling. She refused to answer Smythe's questions and he did the same with hers. She rang off with a frustrated sigh.

Time of the Demon

What was she left with? Special Branch? MI5? But MI5 didn't wear police uniforms. Perhaps the MoD police? She dare not contact any of them for fear of attracting unwanted attention to herself and the paper. But she had established that Hemingway, if that was his real name, belonged in a much more covert world than any she'd experienced in the past.

She rang one of her contacts in the local force. "Jan Barnes from the *Courier*. I'd like to speak to Inspector Parker , please ... I'll hang on."

She turned on speakerphone. While she waited, she took out the framed photograph of Jess and Gina from her handbag, removed its cheap frame, and put it in an envelope. Returning the photo to her bag, she threw the frame in the bin.

Inspector Parker's voice boomed from the speakerphone. "Afternoon, Jan. How can I help you?"

She picked up the phone and put it off speakerphone. "Hi Ron, I'm just trying to get up to speed on the incident at the Half Moon Inn yesterday evening. Come on, it was a UFO that crash-landed, wasn't it? ...A *hoax*? How d'you mean? ...Two bored bar girls having a laugh? That's not what I've heard! ...You're considering charging them for wasting police time? So we're supposed to go around with our eyes shut now and not report anything suspicious? I've a good mind to put that in the paper! ...Oh, case closed, is it? And whose decision was that? ... I'm *not* being difficult, I'm only trying to do my job–and that's to publish the truth!"

Had she compromised Jess and Gina? Would Parker make the connection and realise she must have spoken to them? Would he talk to his superiors? In what was beginning to look like a very serious case, should she alert the girls to the attitude of the police? Before she reached a decision, Russell stuck his head around the door.

"Busy, Jan?" He offered his usual exhausted smile.

"Never too busy to speak to you."

"Good. I'd like a word. Pop into my office in a couple of minutes, please."

She decided not to contact the girls. They'd just have to say the reporter was lying. She felt they were smart enough to do that. The Half Moon piece had to be written though, but from her own point of view, omitting mention of the girls. She hopped to her feet with fresh determination and headed for the editor's office.

Russell smiled wearily. "Take a seat, Jan."

She perched on the edge of the nearest chair. Russell glanced over, then shifted his gaze to a point on the wall a little above her left shoulder, his usual focus of attack. "Please don't hate me for this, Jan. But I want you to lay off the Half Moon thing."

She'd had enough. She felt her anger rising and made no attempt to contain it. "Give me two good reasons why I should!"

Russell put on his apologetic face. "I just want you to take my word that there's no mileage in it."

There was a touch of helplessness in her editor's hollow smile. But she had no sympathy. "Don't you want to sell papers?" she asked in exasperation.

He shook his head. "Not like this."

"I'm within hours of a scoop! It's a hell of a first for the *Courier*!"

"Nevertheless, you'll have to lay off. It's official." He made a fleeting attempt to appear enthusiastic. "I want you to cover the fire at High Barn Farm. Looks like arson. Police investigators are up there now. Take Alec and his camera."

"Who's been leaning on you, Russell?" she asked angrily. "He's not called Hemingway by any chance?"

"You know very well, Jan, if I was the owner of this newspaper things might be very different. Sadly, I have to play by other folks' rules."

"In other words, you don't want to wreck your retirement," she said sourly.

He looked hurt. "Steady, Jan. No personal attacks, please. If you were in my position, you'd have to do the same."

She sighed loudly. "Arson at High Barn it is then. Now there's a bit of really hot news."

He returned her sarcasm: "I don't doubt you'll extract the most heat you can from it."

She was about to slam out of his office, but changed her mind and turned in the doorway. "So far you've only given me *one* reason for laying off the Half Moon thing."

* * *

When Jan and Alec, a young press photographer, got up to High Barn Farm, they found the badly fire-damaged remains of a remote and long-derelict farmhouse, with a police forensics team combing through the debris.

A lanky uniformed constable commanded the gap where a front garden gate had once been. She learned from him that the place had been occupied by squatters. On the night before the authorities were due to evict them, they'd torched the place and disappeared.

Her growing distrust of officialdom caused her to feel sorry for the squatters. She decided to write a piece giving the situation from both sides and also mention the prohibitive price of property in England. People had to live somewhere and, after all, the owner of High Barn was an affluent farmer who was also a local magistrate. He couldn't lose. He had two other farms and still owned the land the burned-out house stood on. And he'd collect the insurance, for sure.

And the squatters? They had to take their chances, like poor folk everywhere. In such an imbalanced society, squatters may well be the future... Russell would disapprove of the piece, but he might let it pass.

While Alec took photographs, she retreated to her car and phoned Greg. "So here I am, sent into the wilderness. No Hemingway, local force in denial, case officially closed, big cover-up. I feel like screaming."

Greg was also in his car, parked in a lay-by on a lonesome country road. "Apparently the county's police have been on high alert for the past week. Why? Because they're expecting hordes of little grey men in flying machines. Don't ask me who started that story, but it's one reason why Hemingway had to get to the inn ahead of emergency services. And," he added wryly, "ahead of people like you."

"So it *is* some kind of secret military device?" She could hardly believe she was hearing her own voice asking the question.

"I'm pretty sure of it. And local law enforcement had to be kept in the dark."

"But Hemingway got there so fast. He must be local."

"Not necessarily. They might have been physically tracking it."

"The chopper could have been, but surely not the cars?"

"Hemingway might have been waiting for the device. Even if it went off course, they were obviously close to the target area, or the local police would have arrived there first."

His words chilled her to the bone. "Target area?" she echoed softly.

"Some MoD site. It can't be far away from where the light came down."

"You think it was some kind of military experiment?"

"What I think is far too sensitive to talk about on mobile phones. By the way, yours might soon become insecure. Please change it asap or we'll be out of contact." He rang off and pulled out of the lay-by.

Just as Jan's phone call ended, Alec jumped into the passenger seat. "Got all I need, Jan. How about you?"

"I think I need a new head," she replied quietly.

*　*　*

The bedside clock showed 1.30 a. m. Jan tossed and turned, in the grip of a dream.

Fleeting images of police vehicles, flashing blue lights, a whirling helicopter's searchlight. Jess and Gina dance across an expanse of deserted tarmac with two sharp-suited men. A range of low buildings occupies the background. The girls give Jan knowing looks as they sweep past and spin into the distance.

Superintendent Hemingway strides towards her across the weed-lined tarmac. He reaches into a pocket of an anonymous uniform and produces a glowing sphere of bright white light. He extends the light, as if offering it for her inspection.

She peers at it. A figure is discernible within.

The figure writhes, as if suffering intolerable agony, trapped in the sphere of light. She realises that the figure is none other than herself.

Jan awoke with a start, staggered to the window, and looked out. In spite of urban light pollution, from her top-floor flat she could see the moon through tufts of broken cloud. Bare trees in the park opposite rattled autumnal branches in the wind like witch doctors casting bones. There wasn't a UFO in sight.

For the first time in her life, she began to doubt the truth of her own perceptions. She almost convinced herself that the solid floor she stood on was changing under her feet, becoming water, or air–and she was going to fall through any moment. The only thing that had so far prevented her fall was the belief that the floor was indeed solid.

What happened when belief was truly suspended? What happened to normality? She had the overwhelming feeling that the world she'd always taken for granted had begun to shift sideways, into something nameless and incomprehensible.

She sat at the kitchen table with coffee and buttered toast. She could clearly remember the dream and its imagery filled her with foreboding. Another odd factor in what was already a deeply disturbing experience: she thought she recognised the setting.

That range of low buildings belonged to a site that had been requisitioned in the Second World War for use as an emergency air strip and local authority bunker. The site lay among farmland barely five miles to the north of the Half Moon Inn. She'd assumed the place had been abandoned, as so many had been, but perhaps that wasn't the case.

She wondered if the dream was some kind of warning. Fear lurched in her stomach.

Taking her notebook from her handbag, she flipped through the pages until she found Gina's hastily jotted mobile number. She keyed the number into her new mobile, but all she heard was three beeps, followed by a continuous flat tone. She tried again, with the same result. Damn! Was the phone out of commission?

She tossed the mobile into her handbag, finished the now tepid coffee, slipped on her coat and shoes, and hurried out. Ignoring Greg's warning about hidden cameras, she went straight to the girls' flat and tried the doorbell. No response. She didn't care that she might be watched. She feared for the girls' safety and had to help them get away and, if necessary, go into hiding.

She tried again. Nothing. Was she already too late? She peered through the letterbox, but saw only carpet and skirting boards. The carpet, she noticed, was a different colour and in much better condition than the one she'd seen on her previous visit. What the hell was going on?

She placed her mouth close to the opening. "Gina? Jess?"

Silence.

"Jess? Gina? It's Jan from the *Courier*."

A door opened down the corridor. "Shit", she thought aloud, "I've woken people up."

A brawny tattooed guy in ash-grey joggers and black singlet stepped out. She braced herself for a tirade. "They've gone, love."

The warm friendly tone didn't fit with the hour of the night or her stereotypical image of muscles and tattoos.

"Gone?" she blurted out. "Where?"

Her recent impression of normality's impending disappearance was blocking rational thoughts.

The brawny guy waved an arm. "Go in and see for yourself, love. The door's open."

His words brought her back, like a bridge, to her usual decisive self. She tried the door, which was indeed unlocked. She stepped cautiously inside and was shocked by what she found–which was, in fact, *nothing*. The girls' memorabilia and personal possessions were gone. The rooms were bare, freshly repainted, and newly carpeted. Even the furniture had been removed, although it had probably belonged to the property owner. It was as if Jess and Gina had never set foot there. Had they been contaminated in some way? Was this the reason for the radical clearout?

The brawny guy's voice made her jump. "Called on 'em a couple of hours back. I thought they were bound to be in. Owed me money, see. Found it just like this. Couldn't believe it. Changed the place completely and I never heard a thing!" He looked knowingly at Jan. "Owed you too, did they?"

She shrugged. "A fair bit, as it happens." She wasn't going to prove a soft touch.

Had there been a hidden mic in the flat? Had Hemingway & Co heard everything the girls had said? Maybe she was also a suspect? Perhaps it was only a matter of hours before the suits picked her up.

The brawny guy scratched the back of his thick neck as they stared at the empty living room. "It's like the whole place has been bagged up and whisked away by some kind of black magic. It don't seem right to me. Whoever did this, you don't want 'em in your life."

Jan, in complete agreement, said nothing.

4

At eight o'clock that morning, in the city to the east of the Half Moon Inn, Jan and Greg strolled around a small lake in a large municipal park. He threw grain to the ducks and passed some to her.

"Be natural," he said with a jovial smile. "We're here to feed the ducks."

She didn't know whether to laugh or to take him seriously. "Are we being followed—or are you just paranoid?"

"It's always best in a public space to be doing something normal. That's one way to remain invisible. If we feed the ducks, people will watch the birds, not us."

Yes, she thought, blend in, be a chameleon. The unobserved observer. A way of life she might have to cultivate. They walked on a little way and threw more grain.

"So we've lost the girls?" he asked casually, watching the ducks.

"They've gone. I was too late to help them. Not that I had a clue what I was going to do."

"Typical."

"What is?"

"Everything removed. Place transformed. Occupants disappeared." He shrugged limply. "It happens. But new paintwork and carpets seem excessive."

"They owed money. The locals will think they've done a runner."

"That's a good conventional explanation. They'd never believe the truth anyway."

"What *is* the truth?"

"It could be something so staggering that even a couple of years ago I'd have had trouble believing it. The property's probably contaminated. But by what, of course, we don't know."

"So the girls could be sick? They did have very inflamed eyes."

"Typical again."

They continued walking in silence, then stopped and threw the last of the grain.

"The inn's closed and boarded up," he informed her. "I drove past earlier. The police tape's gone, but there's a DANGER KEEP OUT sign on the gate to the field."

"I'm surprised you went to look. I thought you had a thing about surveillance cameras?"

"Questioning witnesses is one thing. Looking at field gates is another. Anyway, there was no one lurking with binoculars. At least, not so far today."

"So the inn's contaminated?"

Greg nodded curtly. "Almost certainly. But the field behind the inn will be the centre of any heavy residues. At the time of the incident, the police didn't set foot in the field, did they?"

"Apart from Hemingway and a uniformed robot they stayed in their cars," she confirmed.

"They won't want anyone near the place for years. The MoD might even buy the property through some proxy company. Then just leave it empty. It depends on the level of contamination."

Jan thought about the unlawful tenants at High Barn Farm. "It might attract squatters."

He shrugged. "Bad luck for them. Burning down the place might be the best solution."

She had the feeling he was leading her into very dark territory. "This is getting creepy."

"You can drop out any time you want. It's not too late."

"Is that a warning?"

"Beyond a certain point there's no way back."

"How will I know when I've reached it?"

"You'll know." He regarded her intently. "Are you in?"

She wasn't sure. But was she going to spend the rest of her life on a provincial newspaper? The incident at the inn was forcing her to make a life-changing choice. With a shock,s she realised she might already be past the point of no return. She wanted desperately to know what had happened to the girls. The idea of their unjust suffering was outrageous. Her social conscience had been awakened. How dare these anonymous powers invade folks' lives–ruin them and never be held accountable! Gina and Jess were collateral damage of so-called peacetime. She *had* to oppose this.

"I'm in," she announced decisively. "I can't go back to reporting on official openings and society weddings."

He gave her a searching look. "Great. But whatever happens, remember never to lose your sense of humour. It keeps us grounded. It's the surest way to maintain sanity."

She absorbed his advice. "So what's the next move?"

"We should have a closer look at UFOs. Take a little trip into their world. I need to make contact again anyway."

"Where *is* their world?"

Greg gestured with both arms. "A million miles out there and just beyond our noses. Busy tonight?"

"Nothing planned ... as yet."

"Keep it that way. We're going to take the wildest drive of your life!"

* * *

They headed into hill country, with Greg behind the wheel of the Audi. The car clock showed twelve midnight.

"How do you find a UFO?" she asked, feeling suddenly apprehensive.

"You don't." He shot a quick smile. "They find you. But some areas are better for making contact than others."

She was beginning to have doubts about agreeing to the trip. But this was the direction her investigations were taking her. Somehow she had to hang on and see what happened–and try to find something to laugh at along the way. However, at that moment, laughter seemed as unlikely as sighting a UFO.

"Where d'you think they come from?" It sounded like a childish question, like something from *Alice in Wonderland*.

"From their own world. It's closer to our reality than you might think. Only the thickness of a wafer away."

He seemed so calm, as if they were simply taking a trip to photograph owls, or watch a meteor shower.

"They're not from outer space?" The question appeared ludicrous when she heard herself ask it, as if she'd questioned where March Hares kept their boxing gloves.

He continued in the same unruffled manner, like an old-fashioned family doctor reassuring an hysterical patient they would soon be better. "You have to abandon linear thinking to get close to this. Then you realise all the worlds co-exist. As someone once said, they're like blades of grass in a field."

"Most folk would find that idea hard to live with." As she spoke, she felt the first stirrings of dread, like doing your first bungee jump and wondering if you'd survive the leap. And this leap, in a very different way, might be even more dangerous.

"It's tough to dump your old mindset to make room for a new one. Without doubt, it's one of the hardest things you'll ever do." He could have been reading her mind.

Well, she'd just have to hang on till she could believe at least six impossible things before breakfast. She glanced out the car window, idly wondering where they might end up. They were travelling through a moorland landscape, with gorse bushes and birch trees along the side of the road. It all seemed quite ordinary.

"You have to remember," Greg continued, "they can get here, but we can't get there. At least, not without help."

He pulled into a lay-by and took a drink from what looked like a bottle of spring water. He took a second bottle from the glove compartment and handed it to her. "Want some refreshment?"

She hadn't had a drink for hours, so she accepted it and took a good long swig. "Ugh–it's bitter! What is it?"

"A traditional herbal mixture. It'll put you into a mild ASC very gradually."

She looked at him in alarm. "Do I need to be in an altered state of consciousness?"

He smiled soothingly. "We both do. Only adepts can get to otherworlds at will. Keep the bottle. I've a suspicion you'll need it."

Jan stared uncertainly at the anonymous bottle. What would it feel like to be in an altered state? Would she lose control of all reason? Would she be able to react to danger? She wished she hadn't drunk the stuff. She'd never done anything so rash before, not even at student parties.

She'd been too trusting of this seemingly good-natured stranger. Who was he? What was his background? Did he lure unsuspecting females to their deaths on the moors while entertaining them with wild talk of UFOs? She put the bottle into her bag, resolving to throw it away as soon as the chance presented itself.

They drove on slowly through rough country. Heather, bracken, and wind-blasted larches lined both sides of the narrow road. They looked a little odd, as if she was slightly drunk, but she didn't feel intoxicated. She could see a sprinkling of stars and a few moonlit clusters of cloud drifting along the horizon. They looked the same as always, but were different in some unaccountable way. No town lights could be seen, suggesting they were far out into high country.

She thought she must have nodded off for a moment, or experienced a brief lapse of awareness, because all at once she found her world had entirely changed. A bright orange light seemed to hover in the distance directly ahead.

"What's that?" she asked, feeling no fear, only a compelling sense of curiosity.

"I'm seeing an intense orange light," he said, without a trace of excitement or apprehension.

"So am I," she stated.

"Just making sure we're seeing the same thing."

The light approached, hurtling toward them at stupendous speed.

"It's going to hit us," she cried out, recognizing that her fused sense of surprise and terror was matched by a feeling of wonder.

"It won't," he said calmly, slowing down. "Just keep watching."

The orange light careered towards them, streaked over the car and into the distance behind.

"It's faster than an airforce jet," she exclaimed in amazement.

"It's coming back," he advised in the same calm tone.

The light, now a swirling orange-and-blue disc, buzzed past again, passing low over the car, then hovering above the vehicle for a few moments before speeding into the distance and disappearing.

"Incredible!" She was overwhelmed by a sense of awe.

"If that was a lookout, we've been sussed." He slowed the car even more, searching for somewhere to pull off the road.

"You're saying that light has intelligence?" she asked in wonderment.

"Correct," he replied. "But remember, it's not human intelligence."

"It's as easy as this then? In an ASC, you just drive out of town and start seeing UFOs?"

"I've been doing this for a while. They seem to recognise me now, if that's the right word. I get buzzed pretty often, but I don't know what it is they pick up on."

Pulling the vehicle off the road, he stopped behind a low dry-stone wall and cut the engine. "This should keep the car fairly well hidden. So much for intelligent lights in the sky–in UFO parlance LITS. Mostly innocuous stuff."

"You're suggesting there's more?" she asked, fascinated.

"Much more. Most folks don't get any further. Some of those who do go deeper get stuck in some kind of ego trip, feeling they've been singled out as special. Often they come to grief. Serious researchers are dismissed as flaky because of the freaks who get blown away by their encounters and receive media attention. So be warned. As the poet said, humankind can't bear too much reality. At least," he added, "not this reality."

They got out of the car and looked around. The stars had disappeared and a hazy glow filled the night sky. Jan couldn't remember when this change had taken place, whether it had been gradual or if it had happened suddenly. She resolved to be more observant going forward.

They followed a narrow track lined with bracken and stunted hawthorn bushes. It was exceptionally quiet.

Even though they must have been a thousand feet above sea level, there was no wind, not a breath of movement in the air. And there was no traffic noise. No headlights on the moortop road, no muffled drone from the city. It was like being on another planet.

"We're in their world," he said quietly.

"Modern life is very intrusive," she said thoughtfully. "Not many centuries back, the transition between worlds wouldn't have seemed so extreme."

"That's true," Greg replied with a nod. "But the Church had made most folks fearful of anything that might be termed *supernatural*. Now it's linear rationalism that gets in the way. Rationalism has its place, but so has intuition and mystical vision."

They followed the track towards slightly higher ground. Walking seemed to take much less effort; it wasn't quite like floating, but it didn't seem to be using any physical energy.

"What fuel are we running on?" she asked, intrigued. "It's not physical."

"We possess many levels of subtle energy," he explained. "But we haven't developed machines that are sensitive enough to measure them." After a thoughtful pause, he added, "Maybe that's for the best."

The hazy glow was dissipating. The night sky was visible and Jan could hear the stars hissing and crackling, as if she was standing in the Sahara Desert atop the Grand Erg Occidental. There seemed to be many more stars than usual, so dense she felt overwhelmed.

Shocked, she realised these took their place among the stars of a *different* world.

"Watch and wait," he advised. "Be alert."

They kept their eyes on the shimmering horizon, turning slowly in a complete circle.

"See there!" he exclaimed, pointing.

Different coloured lights appeared: yellow, blue, orange, red. They rose and fell in formation, and kept it up for what Jan felt, in the world of physical time, would have been no more than a couple of minutes. Then they streaked away at great speed and vanished.

"It's like they were putting on a show for us." She was certain she'd spoken the words, but realised she must only have thought them, like in a dream, but in some indefinable way not quite the same. Had they been telepathically communicating from the start?

"Don't allow yourself to be flattered." She felt her mind receive his reply. "Whatever they do it's only for their own reasons, which are unfathomable to us. As I said, their intelligence is not human. And it's infinitely devious."

The bracken ended and they found themselves at the entrance to an abandoned quarry. Old workings occupied several terraced levels across different rock faces. Trackways led down and extended across the quarry floor, where they entered derelict buildings that stood eerily silent in the windless night. They sat on flat stone slabs among the rubble and weeds at the entrance.

Time of the Demon

It was so like the normal world, Jan thought. It *was* the normal world. But, at the same time, it possessed atmosphere and energy that emanated from somewhere else ... an *otherworldly* somewhere else. It was as if different worlds overlapped at certain geographical points. She found it intellectually difficult to explain, because language was mostly a tool of the rational mind. Better not try, she thought. Just be open to the experience.

A light, flashing alternately egg-white and grass-green, appeared above the quarry, transforming the landscape into an eerie bas-relief. In the nearby distance she noticed a large cat-like creature prowling through the debris scattered along the quarry floor.

"It looks like a puma." She had no fear, only fascination. She knew that Greg had seen it too.

"Watch how it moves."

She received his words as if they were a recollection replaying in her head.

The cat-like creature slunk with liquid movements more suggestive of living energy than physical substance.

"Is it real?" she asked.

"It's real in its own world. When it appears in ours it's more like a phantom. That's why, when folks try to hunt them, they can't be shot."

"Both worlds are here? Right now?"

"And also others we know even less about."

"I feel privileged. And terrified."

"Don't let it go to your head. This is only a mild ASC. A full-blown altered state would be tough to live with. The rational mind would be overwhelmed and might not fully recover. Like I said, reason has a crucial role to play in our lives. To ditch it permanently is inviting disaster."

Mesmerized, they watched the puma and the flashing light. The realisation that this light and other similar forms had intelligence suddenly hit her like an electric shock.

"Are you okay?" Greg asked under his breath. "I felt something happen to you."

"I'm all right. Things are just beginning to dawn on me. There's no way I can prepare myself for them."

In the depths of a derelict building the hideous figure of Owlman appeared, observing them. Jan and Greg were unaware of its presence.

The white and green light started to pulsate, then rose at great speed and shot into the starry sky. The puma also disappeared, as if it had stepped through an invisible curtain.

"I think it might have changed worlds," he answered in reply to her silent question. "Do you want to follow it?"

"No." She shook her head. "Definitely not. I've seen enough for now."

He glanced at the sky. The moon had appeared, racing through a mass of broken clouds. "Things are changing." He spoke the words aloud; she saw him do it. "The ASC is beginning to wear off. We should go."

They were back at the Audi in what seemed no more than the briefest of seconds, as if they had replaced the laws of time and space by an act of will.

"I can hear traffic," she realised suddenly.

"What does that tell you?" he asked, eyeing her closely.

"We're back in our world."

"Did you notice the transition?"

She thought a moment. "It was seamless."

He laughed heartily. "Blades of grass in a field, right?"

"So that was leaving normal?"

"And now you know normal is only one very limited reality among many."

They headed back towards the town, driving slowly between wide laneside verges covered with heather and dotted by birches. This was her familiar, but unfamiliar world: tree, flowering shrub, wayside boulder – gatekeepers of mystery. Traffic overtook them, going towards town. She glanced at the car clock: it was 6.45 a.m.

"People are rushing to work," he remarked casually.

She pointed to the clock. "We've been up here more than six hours. It only seemed like an hour, or maybe two, at the most!"

"Evidently time in other worlds moves at a different rate," he observed, then laughed. "Perhaps, in some worlds, time will run backwards and we could return to the years *before* we started out."

She pondered for a while. "You said those lights had non-human intelligence. Is it superior to ours?"

"It's different. It's not a rounded moral intelligence like ours. Don't expect compassion or sympathy from entities in that world. They might try to feign it, but it simply doesn't exist there. And don't try to explain what you see. Like I said, human reason and their world don't connect. That's why you need your sense of humour to stop them ensnaring you with spectacular visions and grandiose promises they never have any intention of fulfilling."

She was still mulling over Greg's comments when the city appeared, spread out below. The familiar world again. But did we even know this world? Or were we simply blinded by its seeming permanence that prevented us from seeing beyond it?

A new thought struck her. "We should try to find out what's happened to those two girls."

"Yes, we must," he agreed. "I have a contact, a friend of a friend, who might be able to help us."

5

Jan and Greg drove through a large well-kept Cotswold village. Stone-built cottages surrounded the village green, which was dotted with mature oak and horse-chestnut trees. The trees seemed strange and mysterious to Jan without their friendly clothing of summer leaves. She had taken them for granted, never really seen them. Now they appeared faintly sinister, as if they knew many dark secrets.

"The essence of English charm, don't you think?" Greg's voice interrupted her thoughts.

"It's too twee for me, I'm afraid. Don't suppose anyone but yuppies can afford it."

"Well, the yuppie we've come to see has an extraordinary gift. So don't judge the contents by the packaging."

His put-down stung her. She was still smarting as he parked the Audi and she followed him dutifully up a winding garden path, bordered by shrubs she couldn't name, to the front door of a Virginia-creeper-clad cottage.

Five minutes later, they were seated in comfortable armchairs in an oak-beamed sitting room. Heather, an attractive dark-haired lady in her late forties, brought in a tray with tea and a selection of chocolate biscuits.

"It's a little snack," she announced cheerfully.

"Much appreciated, Heather," Greg replied with a thankful smile. "It's been a long drive."

"I find a light snack is quite relaxing, without actually dulling one's sensibilities. I try to avoid the distraction of physical discomfort when I'm working. It's important for both myself and my clients that we should all quieten our minds and be at ease."

"I completely agree," Greg grinned. "One needs to be quiet to hear the still small voices of revelation."

You ingratiating sonofabitch, Jan thought.

As they nibbled biscuits and sipped tea, Jan slowly came to terms with Greg's excessively deferential attitude. It seemed as if he truly belonged in this picture-postcard village, as if he was taking tea with a maiden aunt. The chameleon.

"Now, tell me how I can help you," Heather said as they finished the last of the biscuits.

It was Jan's cue. At a glance from Greg, she began. "We need to find these two missing girls." She took the photograph of Jess and Gina from her bag and passed it to their hostess.

Heather's cocoa-brown eyes studied it intently. "This was taken recently?"

Jan hadn't a clue, but plunged on. "Last summer holidays, I think."

"Do these young women look very much today as they do here?"

Jan had to think back. "Their hair's longer now and in different styles, but otherwise they're the same."

"You're certain the girls are both still alive?"

The idea that they might not be stopped Jan in her tracks. Greg came to her rescue.

"We have no reason yet to think otherwise."

With a quick nod, Heather stood up. "Very well, we can start right away."

Minutes later, Jan and Greg sat in a small room, which Heater described as the back parlour. White noise absorbed all ambient sound in the semi-dark room.

Heather was seated on an antique ladder back chair behind a screen. The photo of Jess and Gina lay on a small rectangular coffee table with Heather's slender hand resting lightly on it.

Jan was seated at an occasional table in the sparsely-furnished room, a small metal-shade reading lamp at her elbow and her notebook open in front of her. The lamp cast a muted yellow glow over the notebook and the backs of her hands. Greg occupied the opposite side of the table with his laptop, which was on. They sat in silence for a while.

"I'm getting a view of water," Heather said suddenly.

"Is it a lake?" Greg asked quietly.

"No. Not a lake. More like the sea. There are small boats ... dinghies, I think ... and there's a headland, a very big headland. And a bay with a sandy beach."

As Heather and Greg talked, Jan wrote key points in the notebook.

"Is it in England?" Greg prodded.

"In England, definitely, yes."

"South coast?"

"It feels like the north. Yes, definitely, the north-east."

"What can you see?"

"I'm looking at hotels above the beach. I'm going past them into a town ... I think it's quite a small town. It has the feel of one. I'm going down a street."

Jan jotted more notes.

Heather fell silent and her visitors waited while the silence continued. Eventually, Greg spoke. "Are you still in the town?"

Heather's voice was strong, emphatic. "Yes. Another street. I'm having a problem with the light ... it's grown very dark and stormy."

"Can you tell us what you see?"

"Small hotels. I'm looking up at one now ... and it's up several steps ... a tall narrow building."

"Has the hotel got a name?"

"I think it's above the entrance ... but it's not at all clear. There's very poor light. I'm trying to get closer. Ah yes, it's the Waverley Hotel."

Jan wrote more notes as a flurry of activity began on Greg's laptop.

"The Waverley Hotel in a town with a big headland?" he asked, glancing up from the laptop excitedly.

"Yes. The headland's very big."

"I think I've found it," Greg announced, sounding pleased with himself. With a quick smile, he turned off the laptop and got to his feet.

Heather smiled in return and requested they sit down to tea and cake before leaving, which they graciously declined.

"Thanks very much for all your help." Jan was genuinely impressed, marvelling at Heather's ability to allow her perception to leave her physical body and roam freely across the planet. She also felt their hostess was a little self-indulgent in spite of her remote-viewing gift, but she wasn't going to share this with Greg.

"It's been invaluable," Greg added and passed Heather an embossed white envelope which, Jan supposed, contained her fee.

"I'm so glad it worked out for you," Heather beamed. "It's been a pleasure to meet you, Detective ...?"

"Hemingway," Greg said with a smile, ignoring Jan's surprise. Nodding to Heather, he led the way outside.

"Why Hemingway?" she asked as they drove out of the village.

"It's under-cover business, isn't it? What better than to give the name of a guy who doesn't exist?"

"He must exist *somewhere*."

"Then I hope he has a sense of humour!"

* * *

The Waverley Hotel exuded a superficial impression of old-fashioned comfort, with deep carpets, over-stuffed armchairs, and discreet wall lights. "Music from the Movies" played softly in the corridors. But it was a false impression, as the furnishings and decor could lay no claim to real quality.

Jan and Greg took seats in the otherwise empty lounge. He wore a black baseball cap, pulled down low over the forehead, which cast his features in shadow. He sat apart from Jan, as though he didn't know her, apparently absorbed in the pages of *Exchange & Mart*. The initial interview would be hers.

Jess and Gina walked in. They stood for a moment in the doorway, as if assessing the situation. Their hair styles and make-up appeared slightly altered; otherwise they looked the same as before, except that Jess seemed, in some hard-to-define way, to have aged a year or two.

Jan rose to greet them. Greg remained reading, his cap pulled farther down.

"Hi again." Jan smiled as cheerfully as she could.

"Hi. I'm sorry, but I've forgotten your name." Gina appeared apologetic. "The desk guy's got a terrible accent."

He was Polish, the reporter in Jan had already learned. Jakub was managing the place for the hotel's aging owners to gain experience in the English provincial holiday business.

She smiled at the girls. "Jan Barnes." She didn't believe her name was all that hard to pronounce. Jakub had called her Yann, but by the third attempt had managed the J perfectly.

"Oh, yes," Jess said with a smile. "The lady from the paper."

"That's me."

"Who's he?" Gina nodded towards Greg.

"My camera guy," Jan said simply, offering their previously prepared reply. "We're covering a conference further up the coast."

Her explanation appeared to satisfy them and both girls ignored Greg completely.

"How did you find us?" Jess asked, eyeing her curiously.

Jan shrugged. "I'm a journalist. It wasn't all that difficult."

The girls sat side by side on a sofa. Jan returned to her armchair and studied them, smiling amiably. "So how come you're here?" She spoke quietly, making a show of respect for the girls' privacy.

"We were told the inn had closed," Jess said innocently.

"Who told you that?"

"The manager," Gina explained with a deep frown. "That bloody Graham. He paid us what we were owed, then told us we were out of a job."

Jess elaborated. "We were out of work, so we looked on the internet and there were two positions advertised in a bar here in town. We did a Skype interview and got the job, 'cos we've had loads of experience."

"You're not working in this hotel then?" Jan already had the answer from Jakub, but she wanted to observe the girls' response.

Gina laughed dismissively. "In this stuffy dump? We're only booked in for a week."

"We need to find a flat," Jess added, "just as soon as we start working. This place is for oldies."

"Why are you here?" Gina asked suspiciously. "What d'you want from us?"

"Just to make sure you're okay," Jan replied reassuringly. "You seemed a bit upset when we spoke. Your neighbour Bernie was worried about you."

Gina laughed. "We were just very tired. If you see old Bernie, tell him we're all right."

Jess waved her hand, as if brushing away a bothersome insect. "It's all in the past now. Time to make a new start."

Time of the Demon

"You haven't had any more thoughts about the light you saw in the field?" Jan asked casually, keeping her voice low. A glance at her 'camera guy' showed he'd fallen asleep.

"I think we made a mistake with that," Gina stated emphatically. "It was that tricky time of day–you know, not quite night, but hardly daylight either."

"It was probably the reflection of plane lights on the low cloud ceiling," Jess put in with a limp shrug.

Jan pressed again. "Is that what you *really* think?"

The girls exchanged an anxious glance.

"It is," Gina said curtly. "*Really*."

Jess nodded in agreement. "*Really*."

Jan stood up. "Thanks for your time. I'm just glad you're both okay. I hope you enjoy your new jobs."

Jess smiled, Jan thought, with relief. "Thanks. So do we."

When the two girls had gone, Greg rose and made for the front entrance. Jan followed. When they were heading west in the Audi he took off the baseball cap and tossed it onto the back seat.

"You wrapped that up pretty fast. I expected more of a head-on challenge."

"I couldn't see the point. I already knew it wasn't them."

"I'd suspected that–but how did you know?"

"They were good lookalike actresses–and probably well paid–but not quite convincing enough. I can't understand how they thought they could pull it off. They were well prepared, but it was lots of little things. For a start, they didn't look quite the same." She produced the girls' photo and held it briefly before him. "I knew as soon as they came into the room. How, I couldn't tell you; I just did. I thought this new Jess seemed older. And they'd reversed roles. Jess had been the dominant one, whereas it was Gina this time when I spoke with them. And that reflection of plane lights is straight from Hemingway. That was the lie he'd told me. But what clinched it was the name of the neighbour."

"Old Bernie?"

"The neighbour I met never told me his name."

He chuckled. "Clever-clever. You're way better than they are!"

"I wish! Who are *they* anyway?"

"Some covert unit within the security services. Maybe one that's completely under the radar. I can't be more precise than that yet."

She looked worried. "Have I made myself a target?"

"They're obviously taking your interest in the case very seriously, or they wouldn't have bothered to set all this up. One or both of the girls probably had hidden mics and cameras. They wouldn't have seen much of me thankfully. Glad I thought of the hat."

His laidback manner irritated her. "It might be all right for you, but what should I do? I'm the one caught in the crosshairs."

"You could let them think they've fooled you and cool it for a while. Or you could back out now and return to your normal life. It's probably going to be your last chance."

For a moment she was tempted, but it was merely a brief lapse of nerve. She couldn't go back to what she'd already outgrown. "I'm not leaving you to take all the credit. I'm in this for the long haul."

He seemed relieved. "I'm delighted, if for no other reason than I won't be on my own with this. It's quite a load to carry on these male chauvinist shoulders!"

She laughed. "Poor you. Do we keep looking for the girls?"

"I'd like to, but I'm stuck for ideas. Any suggestions?"

"Of course. I also know someone." Someone more reliable than precious Heather she felt like saying, but kept mum. Scoring points with Greg wasn't going to help the real Jess and Gina.

He beamed. "I knew your local contacts would be helpful."

She took out her mobile. "Let's hope he's at home."

6

Cyril let Jan and Greg into the hallway of his well-maintained suburban bungalow. An enticing aroma of cooking—herbs and meat and bread—drifted from the kitchen-diner. He waved a hand in the direction of the smell.

"There was a time when my wife cooked just for the family. Since we retired, it seems she's baking for the entire street," the tall, lean and slightly stooped man explained with a quick smile. "She's making traditional Cornish pasties this afternoon. As much as I enjoy her cooking, I prefer using my free time to engage in more mysterious things."

"Traditional Cornish pasties?" Greg inhaled deeply and smiled. "Takes me back to my youth."

Jan shot him a quizzical glance, but he didn't elaborate.

Cyril led them into a sitting room crammed with books of every size and age; they filled glass-fronted cabinets from floor to ceiling on two walls. "I'm busier now than ever," he continued genially, "catching up with all the books I didn't manage to read when I was teaching. I'm under no illusions that I'm in need of more education myself."

He took a fold-out map of Britain from one of the cabinets. "I start wide and then narrow down," he explained. "It's the quickest way in the long run." Producing a pendulum from his pocket, he laid it on the map. "I've done a lot of this work over the years for the police and private clients." With a sharp glance at his visitors, he added, "But I haven't always been successful."

"You found those missing Sheldon sisters after everyone else had given up," Jan put in enthusiastically. "I wrote a front-page feature on it. You insisted I called you Mr C!"

Cyril smiled self-consciously. "Yes, I found them. But it took me quite a few attempts. I was looking in England, because that's where the police thought they were. It wasn't until I dowsed the map of the world that I realised they were in Australia. As you'll recall, we thought we were looking for living people. But it turned out they were both dead." He turned to Greg. "Their estranged father had abducted them, you see. And he'd shot them and himself four months later in an abandoned mining town in the outback. Tragic case."

"I'm impressed," Greg said. "That's quite a feat."

"The trick is never to have any expectations of what you're going to find. A dowser, whether he's looking for water or missing people, must start with a blank canvas." He studied his visitors shrewdly. "It's harder to achieve than you might think. You have to reach a state of self-absence. A kind of trance, if you will. Every dowser has their particular method. I achieve the state of mind I want through auto-suggestion. Now that I have all the information I need, I'd like to be alone to prepare."

They left him, taking the opportunity to get something to eat, Greg resisting the temptation to follow the delicious smell of Cornish pasties to the kitchen. It had become an unspoken agreement that he supplied transport and paid for the Audi's fuel while she was in charge of food breaks. Jan felt she was on the winning side, but he didn't complain.

"You know, Cyril never charges for his work," she said as they munched their way through a large and very late all-day breakfast in a little greasy spoon she'd known all her working life. "He feels if money is his motive, he's abusing his gift. Maybe that's why he's so successful." That was a dig at Heather. Then she offered a palliative comment. "But I've heard of water diviners who charge by the hour, plus expenses."

"Maybe it depends on whether you think of your gift as given by some external power, such as a god–and that it can be taken away if you abuse certain imagined rules. Of if you believe it's a talent you've developed through your own efforts."

"I've heard of families of dowsers. Usually father to son. Like it's in the DNA."

"Do these dowsers charge?" he asked over his coffee cup.

"Of the two I know, one does and one doesn't. Neither, as far as I'm aware, are particularly religious."

He laughed. "Are we any wiser after this conversation, or do the mysteries of life elude us the more we try to pin them down?"

"You're suggesting we should live in a state of innocent wonder, like young children?"

"Or like mystics," he countered, "open to visions."

* * *

Cyril worked through his maps, reducing the search area until he had a large-scale Ordnance Survey map spread out before him. The photo of Jess and Gina lay at one side of the map while he quartered the area slowly with the cord of his pendulum held gently between thumb and index finger.

Eventually, he was certain. He rang Jan's number and asked them to return to the house.

"I think you'll find them here." He circled an area on the map in pencil. "It seems to be a large building of some kind. I've written down the grid reference so you can find it on your own map."

Greg looked over Cyril's shoulder. "It's at least a hundred miles away. We'd best get going."

Cyril placed a restraining hand on Greg's arm. "I've done this for you because I know Jan and I trust her judgement. I've treated it as a missing persons case without possessing any details. But I can tell you that I believe the girls are alive at the present moment. Good luck."

They shook hands with the kindly dowser.

Jan smiled. "Thanks, Cyril. I'll keep your name off the record, as usual."

Jan and Greg hurried into the gathering darkness ... and the unknown.

* * *

It was after six o'clock by the time they set off down the motorway, with Greg as usual behind the wheel, and Jan studying a road map with the aid of a penlight. After driving for sixty minutes, he turned into a services area.

"Another hour to go," he said. "I need a break to gather my wits."

They sat in silence, drinking indifferent self-service coffee. Finally, he reached into a pocket and passed her a folded sheet of paper.

She scrutinised what seemed to be a list. "What's this?"

"Titles of the best books on ufology. Read one or two if you can. Could help you stay sane in what often feels like a world of total madness." He grinned. "And don't take yourself too seriously. Remember, laughter's a great liberator."

"Sounds like you're preparing me for some terrible ordeal."

"It's more a test of personal equilibrium. This stuff can throw you a bit." He pointed to the list. "That one's a collection of essays covering most of the subject. Good one to start with."

They finished their coffee and continued down the motorway.

"One thing I would emphasize," he advised, "is to be sceptical. In the world of ufology, ninety-nine per cent of the entities you meet will be some kind of tricky customer who'll mislead you and lay traps. The skill is to know the one per cent who are the good guys, the ones who can help you. But it's not always easy to tell them apart."

She laughed. "It's not that much different from this world then, is it?"

"Both worlds are full of takers. Our species rapes the planet and they steal from us. They take blood from our animals and samples from ourselves. It's outrageous."

"You're talking about animal mutilations?"

"The examples are endless. And there's another thing. Never look at UFO entities full-face. Some of them are higher-order demons. Their power will overwhelm you. Try to keep them in the corner of your eye if you can. Otherwise, they'll drain your energy like water from a bath."

They approached a slip road.

"We turn off here," she said.

* * *

They exited the motorway and headed down the slip road that led to a main A-road which, in turn, took them on to a surprisingly wide and well surfaced minor road. After a couple of miles they passed a sign that read Woodlands Hospital. Under the sign was another: NO UNAUTHORISED ACCESS BEYOND THIS POINT.

The hospital, in the centre of a sizeable tract of mixed broadleaf woodland, was aptly named. Greg pulled the Audi a little way into the trees and they continued on foot.

Both wore dark hooded jackets, with hoods raised to hide their features. After threading their way between tall oaks and beeches, they found themselves approaching a large plain-fronted building of functional glass and concrete that might have been twenty years old. The windows and wide tarmaced approaches were brightly lit. The place was separated from its arboreal surroundings by nothing more menacing than a four-foot-high wall of pale quarried sandstone.

Reaching the edge of the trees, Jan and Greg peered cautiously through the bare branches. Above the main entrance were the words Woodlands Isolation Hospital.

"If we assume Cyril's right, then the girls are in there." She couldn't contain her shock and dismay. "What the hell did they do to deserve this?"

"They were in the wrong place at the wrong time. Looks like they became contaminated by whatever came down in that field. Then there's the closed inn and the gutted flat. Someone's being very careful to keep the incident under tight control." He appeared puzzled. "This suggests the military rather than UFOs, but I can't shake off the feeling that somehow it's both."

"Most of the officers at the incident stayed in their vehicles, which also suggests a risk of contamination. If it was carried in some kind of warhead, why didn't it explode? And if it was being conveyed by a drone, why didn't the girls spot wreckage?" She shook her head in mystified frustration. "They said they saw only a light. And it was silent."

"I agree it seemed more like a UFO than a weapon. But, as you've seen for yourself, the behaviour of the authorities suggests otherwise." He looked at his watch. "It's after ten. It'll just be the night shift on duty. We have to chance it."

They assumed there were security cameras hidden in the perimeter woodland with a clear view of the building and its approaches. It seemed impossible to get inside without being seen.

A large shipping container had been left on the tarmac at right angles to the goods entrance, where the doors to a loading bay had been left open. If they could reach the container, they might have a chance.

"Let's hope they don't have an infrared security system," Greg muttered as they left the cover of the trees.

There was no one about at that late hour and they didn't seem to trigger any alarms–unless, of course, they were already being observed on CCTV somewhere deep within the building. They reached the container without mishap, then they were in the loading bay. So far so good.

A narrow door at the end of the loading bay led to a storage area, where off-loaded items stood on racks:

catering supplies for staff and patients, boxes of bedding, regulation white coats and protective clothing. As they slipped on white coats, the thought occurred to Jan that perhaps security was thin because it was considered one of the last places anyone would want to break into. The fear of contamination by some rare disease, even if ill-founded, would put off most people. There would be no reason for breaking in here, unless you suspected an infringement of a patient's civil liberties–and that was unlikely to happen often.

Having decided that the admissions office would be situated close to the main entrance, they made their way through silent, deserted corridors. Although they encountered a couple of preoccupied staff members hurrying into a lift, they located the office without being challenged. The small room contained the usual filing cabinets and desks. No night staff were in attendance as the majority of admissions would take place during the day.

Donning surgical gloves, they tried the filing cabinets, but found most were locked. Obviously, patient confidentiality was paramount. After a ten-minute search, Jan found a drawer of an unlocked filing cabinet containing files marked RECENT ADMISSIONS.

"Got it! Jessica Bryce and Georgina Lovell, admitted yesterday. Patients B42 and B43. Room 108. Guess that would be Ward 8 on the first floor." She read aloud from the girls' slim file. "To be kept under close observation... And there's an emergency number for a—"

He pulled a sour face. "Superintendent Hemingway, by any chance?"

"Who else?"

"That could suggest they suspect—or have confirmed—some degree of contamination. And there's absolutely no chance of us rescuing them. Apart from being caught, we might risk contamination ourselves and I for one can't afford to chance it. Can you?"

"I've spent time with them and I still feel okay. But I didn't drink anything or handle personal items like towels." A new thought struck her. "What if all this is a front and they're really prisoners?"

He shook his head. "We have to assume contamination. If the authorities wanted them to disappear, they'd have put them in secure detention. Even if we tried to rescue them and managed to get them out of here they might die—and so might we. As much as we might not like it, they're probably better off here."

"As guinea pigs?"

"We don't know that. And even if that was true, there's nothing we can do." He looked at her sternly. "You mustn't let yourself be troubled by guilt. It'll become an undermining influence and prevent you from coping with any challenges you might have to face. From their first sighting of that light the girls' fate was sealed. At least we know where they are. I think we should cut our losses and go."

She accepted the logic of his argument. They photocopied pages from the girls' admission files—both for the record and as a safeguard against future hostile developments.

They turned to leave, but before they could reach the door a uniformed security guard strode in. His look of surprise gave Greg his chance to hit the guard full in the face with a Taser; before he could fall, he caught the burly man and eased him to the ground.

"Sorry, mate," Greg said quietly, "but we can't all be Mister Nice Guys."

He and Jan left the office swiftly.

"We might have fifteen minutes if no one finds him," he said as they slipped outside. "Let's hope there isn't some way they can cut us off on that minor road."

They weren't that lucky. After a few minutes they found they were being followed by a vehicle that had appeared from a side road a mere fifty yards behind them.

"They'll have got the registration number already," Jan said solemnly. "They'll know it's you. How can we possibly escape them?"

"I'm not too worried about that," Greg said dismissively. "At least they're behind and there isn't a roadblock. I didn't pass my advanced driving test for nothing–let's see what this machine can do. Hold on!"

He floored the accelerator and laughed as the distance between the two vehicles increased from one hundred to two hundred metres. They took the motorway link road at 120 mph but, due to very light traffic, the pursuing vehicle kept sight of them and—to Greg's stunned surprise—was able to match his speed. After ten minutes, he realised the chase would continue until the motorway police were alerted and pulled them over.

Jan turned and looked back. "They're still behind us. At this rate, they could follow us all the way to Scotland!"

"No they won't. I've a plan."

A motorway services area appeared half a mile ahead and he turned into it without giving a signal, driving straight into the lorry park. He stopped behind a gigantic trans-European rig linked to an enormous trailer.

"Perfect. Grab your stuff and let's take a walk."

They hurried to the corner of the lorry park where Greg surveyed the car park with night glasses. "I think I've found them. It's a Range Rover with driver and passenger. They're still driving round. Hard to tell under these lights, but I'm sure the vehicle paintwork is pale, sandy coloured perhaps, or beige, but definitely not white. My guess is it's a military vehicle." With a frown, he watched for a few more seconds. "It's pulling round the far side, almost out of eyeshot. It's time we left."

* * *

Greg turned off the motorway and continued on minor roads; it soon became clear that they were no longer being pursued. The car clock showed 0.40 a.m.

"It's after midnight," he observed. "Have you decided what you're going to do?"

"I'm intrigued and very concerned by this whole business. I'll stay on it till we get more answers. And I'll put an article together as soon as I get back."

"Why don't you start a blog under a pseudonym?" he suggested. "See what happens. You might get some surprises."

"Great idea," she responded enthusiastically. "What about you?"

"I have to call in a few favours. You won't be able to contact me for the next couple of days." He glanced at her, concerned. "Be careful, Jan. Don't get paranoid, but watch your back. And if you come across any entities, show no fear, because they'll feed off it."

She inhaled slowly, then nodded. "Tough call, isn't it– to switch fear off if you're terrified?"

"*Knowing* you have to will help. Fear supplies them with energy. Without that energy they've a lot less power. Still a lot more than you, but the fact they're not scaring you will cause them to lose interest quickly."

"You're not talking about tricky spirits, are you, but what you called *higher-order demons*?"

"As far as I'm aware they're the most dangerous of all the entities you're ever likely to meet. Some of them have been known to use UFOs to impress gullible folk and lead them into a labyrinth of deception. They're hard to outsmart because they can read your mind like an open book. The only way to beat them is through an act of sustained and co-ordinated magic."

"Do you think I'm going to be meeting demons?" she asked, intrigued but disturbed.

"We've connected with the psychic energy circuit quite a bit already with our enquiries. Who knows who—or *what*—might materialise from the ether?"

"Don't worry about me," she assured him. "I'll be far too busy writing my blog posts to get into any danger."

"Make sure you stick to that," he emphasized. "I want to be able to find you when I get back. Don't trust anyone from now on, because no one will be who they say they are. That's the best advice I can leave you with."

7

2.50 a.m. found Jan working on her Facebook blog posts. She was far too hyper to sleep. All she could do at this stage was write a brief outline of events, then devise a short list of questions. There were no conclusions, but quite a few hypotheses. By 3.20 she was satisfied she'd done enough to attract potential interest.

She read aloud through the list of main points:

So there you have it, the 'facts' as I have investigated them. We have:
A strange light at the Half Moon Inn that was not a crashed plane or drone.
Two hospitalised witnesses, possibly contaminated, but by what?
A Superintendent Hemingway, so far unknown.
A boarded-up inn.
A field behind the inn with a DANGER–KEEP OUT sign on the gate.
The case dismissed as a hoax by the local police and officially closed.
The press intimidated and gagged.

An obvious cover-up.
SO WHAT WAS IT?
WHAT'S GOING ON UNDER OUR NOSES?
Was it a UFO?
Was it a secret weapon?
Decide for yourselves. Please discuss. Serious debate welcome. (No time wasters!)
This is SmartGirl2 signing off.

Her mobile rang and made her jump. Thinking it was Greg, she snatched it up and answered. But there was only static on the other end. "Hello? Hello? Can you speak up, please? The line's very bad."

She held the mobile away from her as ear-splitting metallic noises filled the room.

"What the hell *is* this?" She rang off, exasperated.

She began work on her article "Mystery Light at the Half Moon Inn", which she hoped to have published as a freelance piece in one of the more serious alternative mags. Before she'd finished the first paragraph, the mobile rang again. With a weary sigh she picked up.

"Hello? Who is this? It had better be good–it's after three in the morning!"

A distorted voice asked, "Jan Barnes? Jan Barnes?" It sounded oddly metallic, electronic rather than human.

"This is Jan Barnes," she said impatiently. "Who are you? What do you want?"

The same ear-splitting noises sounded as before and she rang off in angry frustration.

"Damn," she hissed at the mobile. She returned to the laptop, but several minutes later, the mobile rang again. "Go away," she yelled.

It kept ringing. After a few moments, unable to subdue her curiosity, Jan picked up again. "This is Jan Barnes. Does someone want to speak to me?"

The metallic voice was very distorted. However, in spite of this, she managed to make out some words: "Meet me at ... the place of lights." The last two words were repeated, then more electronic distortion filled her ear.

"Greg? Greg, is that you?" she asked, suddenly suspicious. "Are you all right?"

"Meet me," the voice repeated, "meet me ... place of lights."

The line hummed. She thought she heard the voice again, but the words were drowned out by a sudden buzz of static.

"Greg?" she yelled.

The static intensified and, irritated, she rang off. She resumed work, but stopped five minutes later and glared at her mobile. It remained silent. Saving her work, she switched off.

As Jan hunted for her car keys, the mobile rang and she quickly picked up. "Okay–I'm on my way!"

She grabbed her coat, shoved the mobile in a pocket, and left.

Time of the Demon

* * *

She knew exactly where she was going–the place of lights could only be the old moortop quarry. She drove along the high moorland road, between bracken and wind-blasted birches, as she had travelled the first time with Greg. When she thought she'd reached the right place, she pulled a little way off the road and got out of the car. Dense clouds scudded across the craggy face of the moon. Owls hooted. Bushes trembled in the wind.

Taking a swig from the bottle Greg had given her earlier, she set off. As she walked, she realised the moortop wind had died and all ambient noise had ceased. There were no more owls, no distant vehicles; it was as if the night had been drained of sound— in the same seamless transition as on the previous occasion.

The moon faded as she walked, masked by a haze of rising mist. The scene, as before, was illuminated by that same sourceless glow. It's happening, she thought. I'm in it. A parallel world. She had no fear, only a sense of wonder and burning curiosity.

Walking was again effortless. She drifted through the bracken and briars until she reached the abandoned quarry. Its derelict buildings loomed and gaped.

Sitting on a flat stone, she waited to see what would happen. The haze disappeared, revealing a sky of fiery crackling stars. Suddenly, a misty white light appeared a little way off across the quarry floor. Then the light vanished and a figure materialised in its place.

The being was a tall male dressed in a loose robe, reminding her of films depicting ancient Roman senators. She stared, mesmerised. Then she remembered Greg's advice about demons and turned her head a little to the side, keeping the figure in the corner of her eye.

"Jan Barnes," he began, "I bring you greetings from the world of truth."

His voice was slightly tinny and oddly mechanical, his lips moving a half-syllable ahead of his words, as if two different time frames weren't quite in sync. She was reminded of a ventriloquist's dummy. She had expected to feel fearful, but fascination eclipsed all other emotions.

She found herself unable to move or think; it was as though the figure in the toga-like robe was radiating a magnetic impulse so strong it gripped her in a state of paralysed wonderment. For a moment she felt trapped, and her emotions almost went into panicky freefall–but Greg's advice again came to the rescue.

She had never been in the presence of a being with such power and she immediately labelled him a higher-order demon. Greg's warning that these entities were supremely dangerous echoed in the back of her mind.

"Do you have a name?" she managed to ask. "You know mine. Please tell me who you are." She found she was talking physically, not telepathising, but speaking in a slow and deliberate manner, almost like an automaton. At the same time, she kept his image in the corner of her eye.

"My name is Ashtar," the mysterious entity replied. "I am the bringer of wisdom to those who are ready."

"Am I ready?" she asked softly.

"You have been chosen," Ashtar declared solemnly.

"Chosen for what?" She suppressed a sudden desire to flee in terror.

"To be part of the new world I am creating," he stated in the same mechanical tone.

"Why should I believe you?" Exercising her journalist's scepticism, she quickly began to calm down.

"I am the receptacle of secrets," he announced. "I understand all things: past, present and to come. Ask me a question. You will see I can only speak the truth."

Okay, she thought, I'll play the game. If I refuse, then nothing might happen. I need to see what this guy can do. "What was my mother's maiden name?" she asked. "The name she had before she married my father."

"She was called ..." He paused, she felt, for dramatic effect. "Jardinier."

"Where was my father born?"

"He was born," he offered another dramatic pause, "in a place that does not exist."

She crossed her fingers and eyed him warily. "Why am I here now?"

"You have been chosen for a special task. You must prepare."

She was reminded of the character Polonius in Shakespeare's *Hamlet*–a pompous buffoon. But the image might be deliberate, one of many disguises the entity had chosen to project.

"How should I prepare?" she challenged.

"I will give you eyes to see the world as it really is. Do not trust the man you are with. He bears false witness."

She was prevented from questioning him further as a glow, a bright aura, surrounded him. He began slowly to dissolve within the glow. The light brightened, then blazed. She stood up and took a step backwards, holding up her hands to protect her eyes.

The light faded and disappeared. Ashtar had vanished.

Shaken and confused, she gazed about. Mist started to envelop her as she stood in the silence. "Greg?" she called softly. "Are you here somewhere?"

There was no response. The silence seemed to deepen.

Unseen by Jan, Ashtar watched from a ruined building. As he did, he morphed into his Owlman form.

A sudden burst of red-and-blue light revolved at the edge of the quarry, then spiralled upwards at tremendous speed, and disappeared.

Jan stared after it in wonder.

* * *

Time of the Demon

As she set off back towards the car, she realised that the old familiar world had returned. Traffic could be heard on the moorland road and the setting moon appeared low on the horizon. The few stars she could see were fading fast and wind was shaking the bushes and blowing her hair across her eyes.

She started the BMW and noted that the clock showed 7.30 a.m. She had been away several hours, but it seemed that no more than a couple of hours had passed.

As she drove back towards the town, she began to hyperventilate and shake uncontrollably. She pulled into a lay-by where panic overwhelmed her; she clutched the door handle as if it was a lifebelt. Finally, she wrenched herself from the car, gasping for breath, lurching as if drunk, still shaking. The shock of the confrontation with a very real entity had turned her rational world on its head.

What could she ever believe in now?

Images swarmed through her mind in numbers she couldn't control. Would she go mad? Had conventional life already become impossible? How would she cope? Would she lose her sense of identity? Would she forget who she was? Questions swirled through her brain like the snaking coils of abyss-dwelling serpents, threatening to plunge her into darkness.

A deer that could have been the living archetype for *Bambi* crossed the road and turned to look at her. She stared at the graceful animal and, for a long moment, they watched each other. Its docile presence began to affect her and slowly she calmed, her breathing gradually returning to normal. She stopped shaking and smiled at the deer in gratitude. This animal must be one of the good guys, she thought, remembering Greg's words, a member of the one per cent that could genuinely help you. Or maybe it was simply a young roe deer, hardly even traffic-savvy...

The deer leaped into the roadside trees and disappeared. She drove thoughtfully down the road into the November sunrise. It looked like the beginning of a beautiful autumn day. But her buoyant mood was tempered by the idea that it might be an illusion, an appearance that simply conformed to the framework of her expectations, while the arcane world of demons was a mere hairsbreadth away.

8

Jan, with exceedingly bloodshot eyes, drank a large mug of black coffee. She tried to call Greg, but got the familiar three beeps, followed by a continuous tone. Emotionally exhausted, she had no resistance left to dispel her growing anxiety and the doubts that hammered at her brain.

Who was this Gregory Houseman? Why had she trusted him? She had no sensible answers. He seemed to understand so much about UFOs and tricky spirits, but he could be a demon himself for all she could prove to the contrary. On top of this, she was worried she was losing her wits. It must have begun when she'd seen the light in the field. Then Greg appeared from nowhere. Was he a secret agent working for Hemingway? Was he monitoring her mental collapse as part of some fiendish experiment?

"Who *are* you Greg?" she exclaimed in despair. "Whose side are you on? Are you working for the military police?"

After another mug of coffee she began to calm down and returned to her desk. In an attempt to make sense of the encounter with Ashtar, she starting writing in her notebook:

My mother's maiden name was Gardener. Why would Ashtar give it in French? And my father's village was a victim of coastal erosion. Why not say so? Is Ashtar trying to convince me he's not reading my mind? Because there is surely no other way to know the answers to these questions. And, as I am ever so reliably informed, the human mind is an open book to demons. I think you are one of the tricky ninety-nine per cent Ashtar. Maybe I should replace 'tricky' with the word DANGEROUS???

She tried Greg again with the same result. Frustration and despair swept through her. She grabbed the phone book, ran a finger down the list of names, and jotted an address in the notebook. How stupid. Why hadn't she thought of this before? Swiftly, she headed to her car.

Fifteen minutes later she stepped from the vehicle and walked along a tree-lined suburban street with large houses set back on private driveways. She imagined it in summer, under dazzling sunlight and lush rustling leaves. Whoever lived here must be making quite a stack. She stopped outside a large 1950s' semi and saw Greg's Audi Estate parked on the drive. That Greg had been living only a few miles from her top-floor flat and in a fair degree of affluence–and hadn't even invited her round for a cup of tea–suddenly made her furious.

An unknown middle-aged male answered her imperious knock on the polished hardwood front door.

"Can I help you?" he asked, civility failing to displace a frown of irritation.

"I'm looking for Gregory," she replied tersely.

"Sorry?" The man in the doorway looked bemused.

"Gregory Houseman," she clarified. "He's a friend." She changed course. "A colleague."

"Well, I'm Gregory Houseman," he responded with a deepening frown. "But I'm afraid I don't know who you are."

"But that's his car." It was her turn to be confused.

"I do agree with you there," he replied with heavy sarcasm. "It is indeed my car."

She attempted to control her bewilderment. Then she spotted a pile of unopened mail on a large hall table. "Have you been away?" she asked casually.

"I have," he said. "Not that it's any business of yours. My family and I have just got back by taxi from the airport."

She studied him for a moment, her brain racing. "I think ... I see."

"It's more than I do," he replied, his anger building. "What exactly is your business here?"

"None at all, I'm afraid. Case of mistaken identity. I do sincerely apologise. Sorry to have bothered you."

She retraced her steps down the drive, feeling the man's dark deep-set eyes on her back.

When she reached the car, something prompted her to turn around. A sandy-coloured Range Rover had pulled across the bottom of Gregory Houseman's drive, blocking all exit. Two large men in military fatigues were hammering meaty fists on his hardwood front door...

* * *

Jan pulled into the car park behind a city centre bistro. She opened the window and let the cool November air fan her sleepy face. Ashtar's words came back: *Do not trust the man you are with. He bears false witness.*

She didn't even know the man's real name. "Who the hell *are* you?" she yelled at the dusty windscreen.

An unnerving thought took hold. She was now completely alone, at the edge of a parallel world of which she had no knowledge, a bizarre and terrifying world removed from everyday 'reality' and so-called 'normal' lives. What was this world's true nature? Was it magical, like those moments she'd experienced with the deer early that morning? She was in a state of ignorance, and complete openness. On one side was denial, on the other insanity. Her state of not knowing was a perilous bridge across the abyss.

As she struggled with her emotions, Ashtar, in Owlman form, watched from a nearby rooftop.

She sat at a corner table in the bistro, eating a mushroom omelette and drinking more coffee, this time loaded with cream and sugar. Knowing her senior editor would be worried by her silence, she keyed his number into her mobile.

She tried to sound more enthusiastic than she felt. "Hi Russell. Sorry I haven't been in touch, but I can tell you I'm busy with the High Barn story as we speak."

As she talked, her eyes were drawn to a gaunt ravenous character dressed in a shabby checkered raincoat, who sat at a nearby table. He was consuming an enormous burger, the grease from the thick cheese-covered meat running down his stubbly chin. The man met her stare. She was repelled by the sight of his yellowed teeth that were plastered with flecks of meat.

There was something unsettling about the man; he even frightened her a little. His coarse features had taken on a predatory cast, as if the burger he was devouring with single-minded devotion was the heart of a poor creature he'd pounced upon and killed. Goya's shocking painting of Saturn devouring his son sprang into her mind.

She tried to focus on her conversation with Russell. "The fire investigators are certain the place was torched. So it was arson. I'll email you a draft asap." She made no mention of the squatters and her sympathy for them. At that moment, compared with the Half Moon mystery, squatters seemed like small beer.

Her gaze shifted to the street, where a good-looking guy in a navy-blue tracksuit was jogging across the car park towards the bistro. She found herself smiling in anticipated recognition. But, although the guy looked a bit like Greg, she quickly realised it wasn't him. Her feeling of disappointment was surprising.

When she turned back to look at the man with the burger, she found him gazing straight at her. There was something profoundly disturbing about the intensity of that stare. Was he a demon? Had Ashtar sent him to keep an eye on her?

She struggled to compose herself, trying to focus on

the phone call with Russell, who'd been talking for the last half minute. "Sorry Russell, I missed some of that. It's a bit noisy here. ...Yes, I'm at home, but I've got the neighbours rowing in the yard."

Taking a deep calming breath, she glanced outside and observed the same good-looking guy in the tracksuit still jogging towards the bistro. What was happening to time? Had something slipped in her brain?

She found herself drawn back to the man in the checkered raincoat, who was biting his plate and devouring it with the same obsessive pleasure he'd applied to the burger. No one else in the bistro seemed to notice. Would *anything* wake them up?

To her horror, she realised the man's mouth contained no tongue, but had become an orifice of flickering flames. He *was* a demon. She detested the sight of him so much, she'd have liked to smash the coffee mug into his repugnant face.

She realised Russell was still talking.

"Sorry Russell, I'm not making sense of this. The neighbours are yelling at their kids and the kids are screaming back, and their screams are shattering all the windows in the block. You'd know what I mean if you'd seen *The Tin Drum*. Call you back later." She rang off.

With relief, she saw that the plate-eating man was gone. Then she noticed that the place where he had been sitting was changing before her eyes: the plastic seat and back rest were bubbling into ugly blisters, as if they had been subjected to fierce heat.

How many other demons were passing themselves off as humans? Was the everyday world being invaded? She remembered Greg's comment that demons could get to our world at will. She had to leave. As she got to her feet, she saw the good-looking guy in the tracksuit approaching again. Was he never going to stop? Would he ever arrive?

He was jogging across the street between the car park and the bistro, then–oh horror! A car drove straight into him and she cried out in dismay. She looked again, but there was no good-looking guy anywhere to be seen.

She felt a rising surge of panic. Then she realised she'd been looking at a ghost. She glanced at the customers but, as usual, no one seemed to have been paying attention. Was she the only one with the ability to see phantoms? What was prompting this change? Was it the residual effect of the herbal mixture? Was it Ashtar revealing new knowledge, preparing her for the building of his new world? She felt confused and frightened.

Leaving the bistro, she noticed the ravenous man standing in the street, picking pieces of her smashed coffee mug out of his face. She hurried into the car park. The place had once been a garrison site during the centuries of Roman occupation and in medieval times it had been part of the Jewish quarter, before the Jews had been driven out and massacred. After that, it had seen the burning of so-called witches, who were probably harmless herbalists. Some history!

The present car park and down-market bistro were possibly the safest the area had been for millennia ...

with nothing more scary than the occasional ghost and plate-eating demon.

To her relief her BMW hadn't turned into a pumpkin. As she drove from the car park, she failed to notice Ashtar staring down from the roof of a nearby office block.

* * *

Back in her flat, Jan willed herself to work at the laptop. The wall clock raced around to 9.15 p.m. She finished the High Barn piece and sent it to Russell without checking a single word. Then she turned her attention to a much more burning issue–she smiled at her choice of adjective –the identity of Ashtar.

Eventually she tracked him down in several ancient demonologies. However, he wasn't known as Ashtar, but as Ashtaroth. According to the majority of the demonologies she could find on the internet, Ashtaroth was a demon in the form of a man with feathered wings. Although she hadn't noticed any wings, she had the overwhelming feeling that Ashtar was a mere projection and that Ashtaroth's true form was something else entirely.

After further investigation, she came across an image of Ashtaroth on an obscure internet site as a fiery demon with immense feathery wings and malevolently leering features. She was taken aback, shocked by what purported to be his true form. She read the following: *He giveth true answers of things Past, Present and to Come.*

Well, she thought, that much is true–to a point. She continued reading: *He can discover all secrets. He appeareth in the Form of an hurtful Angel.* She studied the demon's image again and found it impossible to believe that anything but malevolence could come from such a being. And who then was Ashtar but the demon himself in the form of an hurtful Angel?

After more assiduous searching on the internet, she located some recent comments: *Ashtaroth: One of a number of powerful ancient demons. Ranked near the very top of the demonic hierarchies of the ancient world.*

She had the impression that these were characters or powers that had been around forever in various forms and guises. She suddenly realised that this was where the need to offer sacrifices stemmed from. In a creation inhabited by capricious gods and manipulative demons–assuming you could tell which was which–human beings had to spend most of their days placating the one and paying off the other. A real balancing act.

Forget about the monotheisms, she thought. This ancient world had never gone away. She had just encountered one of its senior representatives! And if these characters had been around forever–and if they had constantly been visiting us in their strange lightforms–so much for ufology being a recent thing.

If Greg was here now he could doubtless provide her with references from the *Old Testament* or the *Bhagavad Gita*, which would confirm her new thinking.

She continued searching and came across another piece which described the demons' preferred physical locations: *They inhabit, from preference, the abandoned places of man, unlike benign spirits that dwell in places of traditional sanctity. Demons will invariably cause injury; benign spirits, if approached respectfully, will not.*

She realised that there were two different forces at work here: the good guys in the sacred springs and hilltops, and the villains in the abandoned quarries and post-industrial wastelands. If Ashtar was really Ashtaroth, not just a minor spirit dressed like a Roman senator, her investigation of the strange light in the field had attracted top-level otherworld attention. But what was Ashtar's agenda? Who was he manipulating–and why? And if his motivation was other than human, would anyone be able to grasp what he was really after?

She saw that the future would always be what it used to be; it would always be gods and demons, benign earth spirits and malevolent deceivers. And there were fewer humans around these days who could tell the difference.

9

In spite of her fatigue, Jan slept restlessly. The bedside clock crept around from 1.00 a.m. to 2.15. She was in the middle of an unusual dream. It seemed she woke up in the dream and saw a light under the door to the sitting room. She was sure she hadn't left the light on, so she got up to investigate. Feeling strangely empowered, she walked towards the bedroom door, opened it, and stepped into the sitting room.

Two detectives in sharp suits were ransacking desk drawers and filing cabinets.

"Stop that right now," she commanded, sounding like *Alice*. "Show me your search warrant!"

The first detective, short and squat, shook his head in sad commiseration. "Don't need one, lady. We're above the law."

The second detective, tall and lithe, seemed to have difficulty deciding on an appropriate emotion. He blew his nose and dried his eyes on a very large white handkerchief. He turned to her tearfully. "You go back to bed and let us get on with our dirty underhand business."

"Why should I? What's the sense in that?" she asked accusingly.

The first detective shook his hairless head. "There's no sense left in this world, lady. Just take it easy. Go with the flow."

"What am I suspected of?" she asked, more from outrage than anxiety.

The second detective wiped his eyes. "Whatever it is, it has to be serious. We only do serious."

"My guess is you've annoyed the wrong people," the first detective said, shaking his head so hard he made her dizzy.

"But I haven't done anything," she protested.

"That's no defence," the second detective said apologetically, taking a clean handkerchief from an inside pocket and wiping his streaming eyes.

"What do you know about Gregory Houseman?" the first detective demanded, sticking out his jaw aggressively.

"He doesn't exist," she replied with conviction.

The second detective thumped his fists on the desk like a child at the start of a furious tantrum. "That's what they all say," he bellowed. "But we're not allowed to believe it!"

"You tell me what you know and I'll tell you what I think I know. Okay?" she offered.

Time of the Demon

The first detective shook his head. "We don't know anything. Why d'you think we're here? Anyway, even if we did, it's classified information."

"So is mine," she replied emphatically.

"I've found it," the second detective exclaimed. He took her notebook from a desk drawer and held it up triumphantly.

"That's private," she objected, reaching for it.

"That's exactly why we need it, lady." The first detective stuck out his jaw belligerently.

"It's a democracy–privacy's not relevant!" The second detective waved her notebook tauntingly. "I'll be keeping this." His tears had disappeared and his voice had developed an accusatory edge. He thrust her notebook into a pocket.

"What are you going to do with that?" she asked, suddenly fearful.

"No idea, lady," the first detective replied flatly. "But we'll make sure there's enough in there to frame you."

The first detective got unsteadily to his feet. His facial features appeared to have slipped a little and his neck was not as straight as it should have been. The result of all the head shaking, she thought.

The two detectives hobbled to the door. They seemed to have to hold each other up, as if their life energy was running out.

"Have a good life now. What's left of it." The second detective grinned malevolently.

As soon as they had gone, she rushed to the door but was unable to open it. She hunted for the key, but the only key she could find was much too big for the lock. She hurried to the laptop, but every page she brought up bore the smiling figure of Ashtar in his toga.

A thunderous knocking began, waking her from her dream. Her bedroom was bathed in flashing blue light.

"Damn! The police!" She leaped out of bed and opened the curtains. A revolving orange disc, emitting a pulsing blue light, hovered outside the bedroom window.

"Go away," she yelled at the light. "Just leave me alone!"

Closing the curtains, she rushed into the sitting room. Although she looked everywhere, she could find no evidence of a break-in or any sign of disturbance. Her notebook still lay in the desk drawer. Was this some kind of anxiety trip? Or was it a warning–from herself to herself?

Her mobile rang. She stared at it for a moment then, with great reluctance, picked up. Before she could say a word, she found herself listening to a deep metallic voice, whose echoes and distortion did indeed sound as if it came from another world. "Many are called, but few are chosen. Because few choose to be chosen. And those few do not choose to listen to those who have chosen them."

She rang off. "I'm sick of this gobbledegook." She buried the mobile under a large cushion, dressed quickly and grabbed her notebook and bag. The door yielded to her touch when she depressed the handle.

Although her key was in its usual place in the lock, it appeared she'd not actually turned it.

* * *

In what seemed like the first grey light of dawn she wandered through the town. There was no sign of traffic. Everywhere was eerily silent. Although she knew where she was, she felt a strange desolation had taken possession of the familiar streets.

She entered a pedestrian precinct, where a half-naked male and a topless female were skirmishing. The female had two large tusks, like a sabre-tooth tiger, that protruded from her lower jaw. She was attacking the male with her tusks, gouging chunks of flesh from his blood-soaked body. The male retaliated with blade-like hands, wounding the female mercilessly. A distorted version of Mendelssohn's *Wedding March* drifted thinly through the oppressive air.

The female uttered inarticulate screams. The male growled and roared.

"You see," the male yelled, "you have to work at a relationship!"

"Never give up," the female shrieked. "Never give up!"

They continued wounding each other, splashing through the expanding pool of blood. A typical modern relationship, Jan thought.

"No!" she shouted. "It doesn't have to be that way!"

But the couple were oblivious, preoccupied with their sado-masochistic war.

She moved on and came across a man dressed as a priest, kneeling in a gutter. The man groaned, clasping his stomach in agony. He began to retch, pulling a seemingly endless stream of daffodils from his jaws and stuffing them into a street drain.

He looked at her with eyes that held infinite sorrow. "This is not the life I was born for. I was promised so much, that I might even partake of God's infinite love. See what has become of these promises! I have learned only that we are fools! I know nothing of how Creation truly is. I cannot detect the connections that hold it together. I have been betrayed!"

"By God?" she asked.

"I don't know," he cried. "I don't *know*." He continued retching, pulling thistles from his gaping jaws.

"Who told the first lie?" he wailed.

"Eve," she replied without thinking.

"Wrong," he shrieked. "You're no better than the rest."

"Who then?"

"I don't know," he screamed, tearing his vestments. "I don't *know*."

This is what comes of swallowing lies, she thought. One day you have to get rid of them. However painfully.

She moved further through the precinct. Her attention was drawn to a juggler clad in a Harlequin costume, juggling Indian clubs made of glass. He dropped one and it shattered on the paving, whereupon a homunculus emerged from the debris and scampered across the precinct, giggling with glee.

"Free! Free! Free!" the little figure shouted happily.

A feral tomcat sprang from the shadows and snatched the homunculus in its primal jaws. The homunculus screamed, then fell limp and silent as the cat raced off with its prey.

The juggler turned. "I'm a member of an ancient order that has been holding the worlds in equilibrium for uncountable aeons," he advised calmly. "And now, as you see, I have let it go. If you think this is a sad place, wait for what will follow. I, for one, have no wish to be here one moment longer."

"Defeatist!" she yelled.

"You've no idea," he continued in the same calm tone. "*Homo sapiens* has forgotten everything of real value. I can't bear to witness it."

"You must," she cried. "It's your existential duty!"

But it was too late. The juggler had cut his own throat with a shard of the shattered Indian club. Even the wise aren't smart enough, she thought dejectedly; you have to think a long way outside the box these days.

Gripped by a force of will far stronger than her own, her attention was drawn upwards. Ashtar, in his flowing toga, stood on a nearby rooftop. "Now I've let you see the world as it really is." The metallic echo and imperfect voice-sync were gone. "You see this fallen world," his booming voice filled the precinct. "But we can transform it!"

He morphed into a luminous angel. A responsorial chant, Giovanni Gabrieli's *O magnum mysterium*, sung by the purest of choirs, filled the air. The light intensified, bright as midsummer, and birdsong burst across the precinct.

"A new world will be ours," Ashtar intoned, raising an arm dramatically. "Leave that false witness and come to me! For I am the way, the only truth and the light!"

She couldn't resist him. She felt as powerless as wind-blown rosebay, as if she was enveloped by his will, unable to decide her direction and fate. She couldn't breathe. Blood drummed in her ears. She thought she was going to die.

But she couldn't die could she, because he needed her. At least he was letting her think he did ... for now. Then she felt him relent. *Touché.*

He was still on the rooftop, smiling, holding out both hands in a gesture of benign welcome. "A new world that will be ours!"

She heard the words echo in her head, as if he'd taken control of her mind. There was no way to stop him; she had no will of her own. Suddenly, again, she felt him release her.

"Otherwise!"

The volume and power of his voice flung her back against a shuttered shopfront. The brilliant light, the chanting and the birdsong vanished, replaced by an eerie glimmering twilight.

"Otherwise all will be darkness!" Ashtar morphed into Owlman and disappeared. The transition was so rapid she didn't notice. All light was sucked from the precinct that became a howling windswept desolation, illuminated only by sea-blue corpse-candles flickering along the walkways that led from it.

Without purpose, she wandered through the town. Decaying bodies lined the streets; gruesome ghouls feasted on them and fought among themselves. She turned away from the grim spectacle and darted into a narrow alley, where rough sleepers huddled in bedrolls. She approached one and pulled back the tattered hood.

Russell looked up and offered her a weak smile. "This is what comes of stirring up trouble," he said sadly. "If I was you, I'd claim that pitch over there before someone else does."

"Coward," she yelled in his ear and walked away.

She found a convenience store which, surprisingly, was still open, although its windows and door were heavily barred. Everyone in the place was buying booze, but she bought a jar of coffee.

"You're not going to the party?" the young checkout guy asked, dismayed.

"What party?" she asked, curious.

"*We're* all going," he said. "The world's finished. What's left for us to do?"

"I'm *not* going to the party," she stated defiantly, placing the jar in front of him. "I'm not going to subscribe to your illusions. I'm going to build a better world."

"I remember you now," he said with a sympathetic smile. "You bought coffee here last night."

"Someone has to stay awake," she replied through gritted teeth.

Avoiding ghouls, she made her way through the streets in the direction of her flat. By the time she reached her street, the traffic was moving and normality, whatever that was, seemed to have returned. She added the jar of coffee to the long line of unopened jars that extended across the kitchen worktop.

* * *

Russell was busy at his desk at the *Evening Courier* office. Jan knocked lightly and walked in. The air in the room smelled stale, like an ancient tomb.

She smiled. "I'd half expected to find a corpse."

He looked shocked. "I know I'm getting older, but I hope not that fast!"

She placed a computer disc on the desk. "Alec's pics of the arson thing with my comments."

He looked up defensively. "I'd like you to cover the opening of the new shopping mall. The mayor will be there, plus most of the local council. It's going to create a lot of new jobs, so it's important you write something to celebrate the moment the town starts fighting back against high-street decay."

She gave him a withering look. "The mayor? Wow. In his chain of office and all?"

Russell drew a long breath. "Take Alec. Get some good pics."

"Maybe I'll fetch my Kalashnikov instead and liven things up." She mimicked shooting an assault rifle.

He didn't seem to know how to react to that. "Just get some photos," he repeated, appearing exhausted. "And a quote from the mayor."

"I'll concentrate on the blood and entrails." She swept from the room.

* * *

She attended the opening of the new shopping mall, but it seemed unreal. At one time, not so long ago, she'd have been supportive of the new venture and the local council's efforts. However, things had changed and her allegiance had shifted. In spite of this, however, she decided she should try to maintain her cover as a local reporter.

She recorded the mayor's speech, which contained half a dozen useful sound bites, and Alec got his pics. To her surprise, she'd begun to relish the task, as if she was snuggling back into her conventional persona, like a child under its soft duvet on a cold winter night. But, she knew only too well, it was a feeling of false security.

As she drove back home intuitive prompting cautioned her to park a little way off from the flat. She got out of the BMW with her bag and laptop and began walking. A car parked fifty yards from her door, its two suited occupants very like the detectives who'd raided her flat in the dream, impelled her to stop dead in her tracks. She hastily withdrew, turned her car around, then drove back the way she had come. So much for normality and the value of a cover. Unobserved by her, the occupants of the parked car morphed briefly into hideous demons.

As she returned to the centre of town she thought she'd investigate the second-hand bookshop behind the town hall. She knew the shop had quite an eclectic collection of volumes, but didn't expect to find anything on UFOs. To her surprise they had two of the works on Greg's list; she quickly returned to her office at the paper to read them. Russell, who was busy on his laptop, didn't notice her arrival.

One of the books was the collection of essays Greg had mentioned; she skimmed the pages, trying to take in as much as she could in the shortest possible time. There were essays on abductions, the hypothetical mechanics of flying saucers, various conspiracy theories involving the US and UK governments, a fascinating study placing ufology into the context of folklore, and much more.

It was the folklore piece that impressed her the most and she believed its author was on to something. Rather than seeing UFOs and their occupants as spacemen from distant galaxies, she felt the author was right and that one of the traditional otherworlds was a much more likely point of origin. Like fairies, elves, dwarves, goblins, unicorns and so on, UFOs came from one of the many parallel worlds that overlapped our own.

It seemed that one reason the overlapping of worlds appeared to have reduced was the dichotomy of humanity's mindset. As rationalism gained ground over enchantment, it had become inadvisable to claim you'd seen anything that couldn't be explained or explained away. From UFO 'occupants' to poltergeists, it was risky to claim you believed these phenomena were as much part of our reality as gravity. Added to this there was so much electromagnetic and microwave pollution in the everyday environment it was surely enough to foul up any consistent otherworld experiences.

The more she read the more she realised that every culture throughout history had been beset by phenomena still outside the scope of modern science. Her encounter with the puma-like creature in the quarry brought this fact home to her. So-called alien animals, from black dogs to big cats to lake monsters, had been reported throughout northern Europe and beyond, from the earliest writings onwards. Strange beings had always been with us, from the faery men of Ireland to the phantom Black Shucks of East Anglia.

The second book was an overview of the closest of close encounters with so-called UFO occupants. It was highly entertaining, but seemed to be pretty much in agreement with Greg, that UFO entities, even if they claimed to be benign helpers of humanity, were dangerous deceivers. Clearly, most of the strange lights and their associated entities came from the parallel world of demons, of this she now had little doubt.

What did these demons gain from their association with humans? What were they after? Why was Planet Earth so important to them? Weren't they already immortal beings? Why, in ages long ago, was mankind at the centre of a tug of war between helpful spirits and demons? And why were these demons coming back in such numbers now?

Her troubling thoughts were interrupted as Russell poked his head around the door.

"Thought you were working at home?" he asked in surprise.

"It's the neighbours," she replied simply. "They're shooting out light bulbs with air guns."

He showed no surprise. "Why don't you move?"

"Don't get me wrong, I'm not complaining," she smiled brightly. "I'd join in, but not when I'm working."

Russell took a reality check. "It's after nine. Can I leave you to lock up?"

"No problem, I won't be long," she lied.

When Russell had gone, she went out for takeaway and hurried back to eat in her office. She made sure that both back and front entrances were locked before she sat down to enjoy the meal. But then, she thought wryly, what good were locks against powerful otherworld entities?

Prawn in mouth, she looked around the familiar space, its filing cabinets, telephones, photocopier and scanner. It suddenly became clear that she'd never work there any more. It seemed as if she was visiting a former life, an unimaginably different one, a place where she'd arrived, but not yet acquired her bearings to properly 'settle in'. Perhaps she never would, but she was in it now and couldn't return to a life she'd used up.

Time of the Demon

She finished the meal, but didn't feel like going back to the flat. It might be the most unsafe place of all. She'd have to sleep somewhere, but it had to be a neutral space, one not yet invaded by anyone.

She booked into a nearby guest house, then opened the laptop and began reading her blog. There were several posts:

BrainStorm had posted: *Conspiracy definitely. Trust no one.*

If it was a crashed UFO there may have been bodies. Was anyone stretchered away? Did you see body bags? Someone called SpaceSleuth wanted to know.

Reluctant Earthling posted the following: *There's an undeclared war between western governments and so-called aliens. If we win this war the planet is doomed.*

There was some confusion among the viewpoints, but the fact that these guys were posting at all was encouraging. She read more posts, some a bit weird, others more sane and challenging. The conspiracy guys seemed to be in the majority and that, she felt, was heartening.

The last comment, posted by someone simply called A, caused her heart to skip a beat: *My prediction will come true.*

She stared, dumbfounded and horrified. Demons didn't have computers! If Ashtar/Ashtaroth could invade her laptop, then nothing she wrote was private, no matter how cleverly encrypted. What other means of communication were there? Telephones were obviously a non-starter. Telepathy was out–Ashtaroth could read her mind as simply as a roadside billboard. Carrier pigeons maybe? But even they had to carry coded messages.

A wave of despair swept through her and she turned off the laptop, locked the premises, and retreated to the guest house. As she lay in the unfamiliar bedroom she tried, with the energy she had left, to make things return to normal. She was completely out of her depth, living a life where nothing was as it seemed. She couldn't even return to the flat–she was homeless!

To hell with UFOs and demons! This was outrageous. She was a simple reporter on a provincial paper and *that* was what she had to reconnect with.

But the exercise was futile, she knew from the start. The Unknown was where she had to make a new life. She had to embrace it and—*somehow*—she had to challenge Ashtaroth to reveal his hand.

It was as if she'd conjured him up. At the mere thought of his name, his presence became known, not in physical form, but in her mind. It was the intellectual equivalent of the detectives raiding her flat–she could feel an active force rummaging around in her head, sifting thoughts, weighing motives.

It grew intolerable. She'd read about states of possession, but this was more like mental rape! Then a half-formed idea emerged, one so insane she had to suppress it before Ashtaroth could locate it and render it powerless. She fed the idea into her conscious mind in a slow succession of evenly spaced moments.

She would become an open book ... become his creature and walk that perilous tightrope. It was the only way to go. Her mind was made up.

As soon as she had made the decision, the mental intrusion ceased.

10

At nine a.m. she returned to the office at the paper and wrote the piece on the shopping mall. It felt like her swansong, but she hadn't the slightest tinge of regret. The decision she'd reached the previous evening was all that mattered. From now on, she'd let Ashtaroth serve as guide.

She returned to the books on ufology. It wasn't exactly like meeting old friends, but as she turned the pages she found herself absorbed ... as if she'd been studying the subject for years. This is where I belong, she thought, eyeing a picture of a celestial sphere. This is my new life. The world is a mess, with continued use of fossil fuels and consequent global warming, beyond anyone's power to heal. What had Ashtaroth to offer in the way of a transformation? She urgently needed to know his plan without revealing her deception. An impossible task it seemed.

She projected her hopes in Ashtaroth's direction, thinking of him as Ashtar, the kindly Roman senator. She willed him to receive her thoughts. After a while she felt calm and knew he'd heard. Slowly, she sensed herself filled with his power.

* * *

She was standing at the top of a long flight of steps, addressing a large outdoor gathering. Below were the upturned faces of hundreds, maybe thousands, of listeners. A giant screen and sound system had been set up, from which her face and voice were relayed around the globe. The long campaign had been successful. There had been immense loss of life, but the alien force had finally withdrawn. They would have to colonise a different planet—this one had proven too difficult for them.

She could see the figure of Ashtar in the corner of her eye. He was standing behind a pillar, like a theatre producer in the wings. He was controlling the words she spoke as he had always done and simultaneously syphoning off energy the crowd was directing towards her. But he left her with enough to sustain her constant feeling of euphoria and the self-belief that had, almost of itself, guaranteed victory.

"My friends," she shouted from the steps, "we have won the greatest battle in the history of the human race!"

A resounding cheer erupted from the assembled multitude. She soaked up the adulation, then felt it absorbed by Ashtar.

"We are one people. One people! The rightful inheritors of Planet Earth. It is our world and we have earned the right to possess every inch of it. Thank you for standing solidly behind the Earth First movement. Thank you for supporting the brave leaders who have gained this historic victory. Now we must go forward and make Planet Earth the paradise we all know it could be!"

A great roar went up from the host of listeners. The screen showed crowds of people all over the world leaping to their feet and shouting support. She let herself fill with their energy until she thought she would explode. Then she felt it being sucked out of her by the figure glowing eerily behind the pillar.

"Let us move forward," she cried, raising an arm. "Let us make the New World!"

* * *

She roused from the dream—the revelation—as if waking from a session of hypnosis. It took a few minutes for her churning emotions to settle. So this was Ashtaroth's plan. How wonderful. How completely inspiring. She was one hundred per cent behind it and eager to play her part in his visionary future. She could hardly wait to get started!

Jan filled with stupendous confidence and energy. Oh yes, she thought, this was life. This was how she had always wished to be.

Like a revenant from a discarded world, Russell poked his head into the room. "Message for you. It's just come in."

"Who from?" she asked, thinking of charismatic Ashtar in his toga.

"Someone who signs off as G. It came to the general mailbox. Is your email insecure?"

She shrugged. "Probably."

He passed her a hastily scrawled note that read "change your phone and ring me tonight". A phone number followed.

"It's just one of my sources," she lied.

"You're working on something?" he prodded with undisguised interest.

"It's early days," she replied with an innocent smile.

"Anything I can help you with?"

She shook her head. "Don't think so. It could take years off your life."

* * *

For once she felt famished and tucked into a hearty lunch of chicken au gratin with side salad. She ate in an up-market restaurant as befitted her new role as leader in waiting of the Earth First Movement.

She was finishing her second caramel-infused latte when she caught sight of the checkered-raincoat man walking past the window. She felt like flinging a knife at his face. How dare he follow her? If he was here because of Ashtar she wasn't amused. Didn't he trust her? She was committed to his New World plan and wanted no more spies. To her shock she saw the man wrench her knife from the back of his head as he glared at her. . "Serves you right," she mouthed. "Now disappear!"

That she'd developed an unwanted psychokinetic ability disturbed her. What other unknown talents did she possess? The power of the evil eye, perhaps? The ability to lay curses on enemies? She chose not to speculate further and returned to her office, continuing to read until the early November dusk crept over the city's roofscape. Then she cleared the desk and drove out of town.

* * *

Jan parked herself on a flat stone in the abandoned quarry and waited. A sourceless hazy glow illuminated the area. There was no wind. No sound. The bushes were as still as carvings. It had happened again: the seamless transition.

Ashtar's voice came from behind, making her jump. "You see now that you can shape the new world. You see now that I can give you that power."

She turned slightly, trying to keep him in the corner of her eye. He was in his flowing robe, smiling like Jesus before the multitude at Bethsaida. She could see that his offer could prove very flattering to the egos of many people. Tempted by that persuasive tone, she could understand why less self-critical individuals could fall for it. And even if they realised the trap, they'd willingly succumb to Stockholm Syndrome rather than fight back. Quickly, she buried the thoughts deep in her subconscious.

"Why are you doing this?" Jan asked nonchalantly. "What do you gain from it?"

"*I* will gain nothing. *You* will be the one to benefit."

His persuasiveness was working on another level. Besides ego enhancement, which was easy to handle, so she thought, she could feel her self-possession weakening. He was drawing resources from her, ones she would need to keep his powerful will from swamping her. What could she do to prevent it? Any attempt to outwit him would be read in advance. Regardless, she forged ahead.

"Let's leave this new world for a moment. Whatever your plans for that might be, they're flawed. Most people aren't ready to be part of it. They haven't shaken off the centuries of conditioning. What kind of new world could possibly work for them?"

"I'm not here to talk about most people. You are the one who will lead them. I will give you the vision to inspire them. Fear will drive them into your embrace. You will elevate their minds."

"We're talking about the disenfranchised, the marginalised, are we not?

"They will trust and follow you."

She didn't reject his words as mere manipulation, but absorbed them into her consciousness, to be dealt with later, in relative safety.

Crossing her arms, she glanced at him directly for the briefest of moments. "I came here because I want answers to straightforward questions. Who are those men who look like detectives?"

"They are nobodys."

"Do they work for the military?"

"Not directly."

His evasiveness was beginning to infuriate her, but she tried to keep her cool. "What's that supposed to mean? Do they or don't they?"

He was trying to move before her and she did her best to prevent his full-on presence from overpowering her. She knew through her research that, at any moment, he could transform himself from benign senator to terrifying being or beast.

"They fulfil a function. They don't even know who they work for." His voice was light, pleasant and mesmerising, the once harsh metallic tone confined to the past.

She felt her mind melting, her thoughts losing focus. "I could have guessed as much myself," she said, mimicking his tone and manner. "If you know everything, why can't you answer simple questions? You're more evasive than a politician."

"Ask me anything," he said simply.

"You know what I want to know—the truth about the light in the field. Why not tell me? There's no mileage in playing guessing games."

"Be patient. You will have all the answers you need. I will guide you."

It was clear the meeting was over. She had not been able to draw unambiguous answers from him and he hadn't managed to undermine her independent thoughts. So far, it was a stalemate.

Slowly he dissolved into an aura-like glow and vanished.

She wanted to shout after him, as she would have done with anyone else. Demanding answers from tight-lipped officials suggested they had something to hide. But this demon was new territory. She would have to be extremely smart to get any further with him. If she pushed too hard, he might lose patience and kill her. Trying not to waste vital energy on anger she left the quarry.

* * *

Jan sat in her car, parked in the darkest corner of the little-frequented car park between the canal towpath and the inner ringroad of the city to the west of the Half Moon Inn. The nearest street lights were close to the road; the BMW was almost invisible in the shadows.

She must let Ashtar think he had brainwashed her. She tried to send a direct telepathic message: "I am intrigued by your talk of a new world. We must speak again soon. I am ready to play my part." She had no doubt he would respond. But how?

Gripped by an irrational fear that he might suddenly appear and smother the BMW with his hideous demonic wings, she drove into the middle of the car park, ready to leave quickly if necessary. Was he sending a threatening message, or was it paranoia?

She took her new mobile from her bag and keyed in a number. A muffled voice answered.

"Hello?"

"It's me."

"Are you alone?"

"Of course."

"How are you?"

"Getting paranoid."

"At least you know that. Where are you?"

"In the loneliest car park in the world."

She gave cryptic directions and rang off. Her conversation had been so banal she doubted Mr A, as she now thought of calling Ashtar/Ashtaroth, would have bothered to pay it any attention.

When ten minutes had passed a gleaming Harley-Davidson roared into the car park. A figure in biker gear dismounted and approached the car. The figure removed his crash helmet when he reached the vehicle; it was Greg, looking handsome with a ponytail and heavy designer stubble. She opened the window.

"This is the latest incarnation, is it?"

"Gerry Reynolds at your service," he grinned. "Otherwise known as Big G."

"Feel like letting me know your real name?" she asked with a wry smile. "For old time's sake?"

"How would you know I was telling the truth?"

They laughed.

"A bike's a bit conspicuous, isn't it?"

"Not when I'm wearing this." He indicated the crash helmet. "And it's a great means of escape from dangerous situations."

"How long have you got it for?"

"As long as I want. We've certainly enough time."

"For what?" she asked, intrigued.

"Proof."

She decided to tell the truth and see how he reacted. "I'm working for Mr A, so we have to be extra careful. You'll find his CV in any number of ancient demonologies."

His look of surprise gave way to one of deep respect. "That's incredibly brave."

"There's no other way."

"I guess that's right. Just watch your reactions. He's quick."

"I'll do my best."

* * *

It was a night of muted moonlight and towering horizon cumulus. The Half Moon Inn was a silent block of darkness against the sky. Jan and Gerry, in protective clothing, stood by the gate to the field where the strange light had come down. The rumble of traffic came from the main road and the wind whistled thinly through long grasses by the gate.

"According to Mr A you're a false witness." She tried to sound casual. His amused reaction was unexpected.

"He *would* say that."

"You know this guy?"

"We're old opponents. But I knew him as Ashok. The irony of the name wasn't deliberate, I'm sure. These guys don't do irony."

"And he knows you're with me."

"It seems he does. But that shouldn't compromise your whirlwind romance. Just focus on your new role. Keep it in the front of your mind. Give me a bad press if you must."

"He'll see through your change of identity, even if no one else does."

Gerry shrugged. "We'll have to play it out. I did wonder if you were his target from the start. How many other reporters were here when the incident occurred?"

"None. I didn't think about it at the time. I was just after a scoop."

He studied her face thoughtfully. "It seems you were singled out from the beginning."

"But why?"

"I've no idea; he must have been drawn to you. But don't let it go to your head."

His comment set her mind racing. What could possibly have attracted this demon to her?

"On that night, you're certain the guys in police uniforms stayed in their vehicles?"

"Apart from Hemingway. And the one you spoke to. And the robot on the door."

"It suggests they definitely knew the site was toxic. We won't be here long."

They climbed the gate into the field. He carried a Soeks Quantam Professional Geiger Counter, with two Geiger-Muller counters. She had a notebook and caver's lamp. Halfway down the field she stopped.

"I'm sure this is the spot where the light landed."

"We'll soon find out," he said grimly. "Keep focusing your thoughts on Mr A's new world. We don't want him arriving while we're working."

As they stepped into the area she'd indicated, the Geiger counter's audible clicks accelerated until they became a continuous barrage. She leaned close so her lamp illuminated the counters.

"It's off the scale!" he exclaimed.

After measuring the area and assessing the levels of radiation, she wrote the information in the notebook, trying as best she could to keep her mind focused on the privilege of playing a major role in the future of the planet. After fifteen minutes Gerry decided they had done enough.

Placing their protective clothing into a sealed container in the back of her car, he drove her BMW quickly down the main road. She had set the radio on white noise, hoping it would pre-empt any chance Mr A could pick up on their conversation.

"I'd say the light—I'm thinking of it now as a very sophisticated vehicle—had a radius of between nine and ten metres, " he began. "But the readings are still high outside that circle. And this was most likely only a small experimental device."

She shuddered. "So it was definitely some kind of secret weapon?"

"It's not going to stay secret for long," he said angrily. "We'll have to get this info out there, but it could be too compromising to put on your blog, unless you let me take it over."

She suddenly felt possessive about the blog. "I'll have to think about that."

"Don't take too long."

"I'd like to return in daylight and take photos. There could be visual evidence to back up the Geiger readings."

"Photos can be easily faked. But we can try it."

"Have you reached any conclusions about what's going on?" she asked, eyeing him closely.

"Incredible as it may seem, I think a rogue element in the western military could be working with demons on some unimaginably terrifying project. Am I close?"

"Too close." Excitedly, she told him about her vision of the future, as if she was already selling it to media-led multitudes.

"Wow," he exclaimed. "That's amazing! I really hope it's a success. And I really want to be a part of it. Really!"

Time of the Demon

He was playing the game. But they still had to be wary.

"Mr A's precise plans are far from clear to me. All he'll talk about is this vague new world he's making."

"If it wasn't for that light and what's happened to those two girls, I'd have said that sounds like his usual bullshit." He scratched his temple thoughtfully. "But this time I think it could be genuine ... as far as anything can be with his kind."

He fell silent, refusing to speculate further, but she was pleased he was with her again. Truth be known, she was much more pleased than she'd ever care to admit.

* * *

Next morning Gerry sat on the Harley while Jan climbed on the field gate and took photos, using one of Alec's spare zoom lenses she'd 'forgotten' to return.

"There's distinct circular discolouration on the grass. I can pick it up from here without needing to get closer."

"That might be from heat. Don't suppose there's any sign of blast damage?"

"Nothing I can see," Jan replied with a shake of the head. "The surrounding area looks normal. Any wildlife casualties would have been removed." She pondered for a moment. "So it's a totally silent device and possibly a highly selective killer."

"That looks like a UFO and can be blamed on aliens. An inspired move, thanks to our old pal, Mr A."

"To be used against whom?"

"I dread to think."

"It won't work," she stated emphatically. "It's too incredible. No one will buy it."

"They will if the corporate media goes for it. They've sold other unlikely scenarios. The unbelievable has been accepted more times than you'd think. Holocaust denials got a fair bit of traction. And disinformation on climate change got much more–look at the damage those lies have caused in the last fifty years! Anyway, believing in an alien attack is your job as the inspired persuader of the people."

"There'll be doubters in spite of me. I can only do so much to convince them." With a wry smile she warmed to her task. "I can shout from the rooftops, but they might not choose to hear."

"Believe me, the captive media will sell the idea that we're under attack from space. The mainstream outlets will be full of it. We're halfway there already with all the sci-fi movies, fantasy novels, and videogames, plus so-called extraterrestrial visitations on the fringe. The main doubters will be our parents' generation and older. Most young guys will accept it, certainly in the US, especially when they see convincing images. After all, the West has faked war footage for decades. Even in these extreme times most young people haven't had the chance to become as cynical as we are."

"Mass hysteria. And then everyone's favourite uncles from the military will rush in and establish control. For the common good, no less."

"You've got it. We've been sliding towards this situation for a while. Individual freedoms have been chucked out the window in the name of national security. When the world's population has been reduced by at least sixty per cent, the authorities will announce a resounding victory over the spacemen." He laughed savagely. "Then you'll appear spouting Mr A's script of the new world order." Gerry started the bike. "Let's go. We've been here too long already."

As they pulled past the inn, about to turn onto the main road, a black Mercedes with two grim-looking men in black suits turned off, heading towards the field. The man in the passenger's seat glared at them icily.

"Who the hell are they?" she yelled above the rumbling bike.

"Black Ops guys at a guess, pretending to be MIBs."

He pulled onto the main road and they sped away.

11

Two hours later they were heading south on the motorway with Gerry on the Harley and Jan in her 4x4, trying to keep up. They turned onto a large, busy industrial estate and pulled up outside a windowless warehouse that bore the name A-B Global Distribution & Storage. Gerry opened the loading bay doors with a hand-held remote and they drove in.

As he locked the doors Jan grabbed the camera and laptop from the car. She looked around at the building's cavernous interior. Miscellaneous merchandise, in boxes and crates, was stacked high on steel racks and wooden pallets. Some of the goods were arranged in units, shrink-wrapped in heavy-duty polythene.

"What is this place?"

He smiled. "It's exactly what it says it is: a storage and distribution facility. Goods are shipped all over the world. A friend of mine owns it."

She wasn't sure if she believed him, but there was nothing to be gained from challenging him. He could spin her any tale he chose and she'd never get any nearer to knowing who he was and what was his true background. And it didn't really matter. In a few short days the world had become a completely different place for her; she had little choice but to follow her instincts and deal with situations as they arose.

"Do you live here?"

"I think of it as my HQ. It's quite a busy site, as you've seen. But it's easy to disappear in a crowd." He unlocked a small door at the back of the warehouse. "Let's sit in the office. It's a tad warmer."

She followed him into a room occupied by filing cabinets, a large fake oak desk sporting a laptop, and two typing chairs. A long rack of metal shelving, filled with alternative literature, lined the wall to the rear of the desk. A camp bed, with a bright red sleeping bag arranged on top, occupied one corner.

He switched on an electric fan heater and motioned her to one of the chairs. "Sorry if it's a bit spartan, but I haven't time or inclination to indulge in creature comforts."

She sat on a chair and placed her laptop opposite his. "So this is your hideout?"

He sat and switched on his laptop. "I'm here when I don't need to be anywhere else."

"So you're off the record?"

"I'm not on the electoral register. If we ever get a political system that can create a true democracy I may change my mind. The current system is simply unfit for purpose. So, at the moment, I choose not to vote. I occasionally drive other folks' vehicles, as you've realised. I pay no income tax, no national insurance. My medical records are fifteen years out of date. I'm as invisible as I can make myself."

Her reporter's instincts sprang into action. "What exactly is it that you do? I mean, why such secrecy, such elaborate anonymity? Are you an industrial spy? A double agent?"

Gerry chuckled. "I'm not a double agent. I try my best to be an independent agent. And I can only be one if I'm as inwardly and outwardly free as possible. I'm inwardly free because I owe allegiance solely to the truth."

"Truth's a big subject. It's got so many sides. Which bit's yours?"

"It's sometimes like battling a force ten gale, but I've an insatiable curiosity, a compulsion to find out how creation works. It's led me into some very strange areas."

"Like the worlds of UFOs and tricky spirits?"

"They don't come much stranger than that!"

"Do you always work alone?"

"I have for the last ten years. Before that I was a practising pagan."

A pagan. An authority on demons and conspiracies. A guy who rides a Harley like he was born to it. It wasn't a whole picture, but it was a fascinating start. Jan swallowed a smile and turned on her laptop. "D'you want me to keep going with the blog? You weren't sure about the Geiger readings and the photos."

"I've changed my mind. Put the Geiger info on it. And the photos. Let's stir up the mix and see what floats to the top. You could even try to create the impression that we might be under attack. That should please Mr A. He'll see you're keen to get started."

"I'm running a risk doing this. Mr A can access the blog."

"You could pretend to be using the blog to test the range of opinions and get an idea of the size of the opposition."

"What if Mr A leaves me hanging out to dry? These demons are unpredictable, you know that."

"I don't think he sees you as expendable yet."

She brought up her blog and found there were a lot more comments.

"We might not be able to prove anything yet, but this blog will inform people of what's going on," he advised, looking over her shoulder. "Now it's you who's become the double agent."

It felt as if she was playing Russian roulette. One unlucky move and she might be picked up by the Black Ops guys–or killed by Mr A.

The afternoon passed quickly as they laboured at different tasks. She worked on her blog while he checked surveillance data to see if anyone had been snooping outside the building. No one had. He left for a short while and returned with refreshments.

"Fish and chips. I hate pizza and the Chinese place isn't open yet."

They ate in silence. When he finally spoke, she was surprised to hear him give voice to her own doubts.

"You know, the world of demons has been with us for ever. These entities posing as gods, taking sides, stirring up conflict, allowing millions to die, feeding off the blood and fear. They're at it again. And with climate change it's going to be global. There'll be famine and fires and floods, there'll be droughts and water wars. Cities will vanish beneath rising seas. There'll be millions of refugees, economic and political fragmentation. The life we think we know today will change beyond recognition. How will Mr A's new world take advantage of this?"

She pulled a face. "It puzzles me too. And it bothers me. I'll let you know as soon as I find out." After a moment's hesitation, she added: "*If* I find out."

"I'd have thought unfettered greed over the last few hundred years would have caused enough human misery for him to be sufficiently entertained. Climate crises will take it to an extreme. All he has to do is sit back and enjoy the carnage. He doesn't have to recruit you to some Brave New World escapade."

"But he is, so he must have a plan. I've tried to probe, but he's always evasive. I have to tread very carefully. The more committed I am to his ideas, the more I'll learn." That's the theory anyway, she thought with a pensive sigh.

They finished their meal and as they cleared the desk, she voiced an idea that was troubling her. "We've talked about future horrors. Where are the good guys in all this?"

"They exist, believe me. I hope you can meet some of them one day."

"My blog seems pretty useless when you think what we're up against," she said sadly.

"Don't despair. Your blog increases awareness. And awareness is everything. In helping Mr A, you're getting the word out." He flung up his hands dramatically. "Hurrah for Mr A! He wants to change the world. Just be sure to let everyone know what a wonderful thing that is. You must play your part, you *must* be enthusiastic."

She smiled ruefully. "You'd make a much better double agent than me."

They continued working. Eventually she shut her laptop. "Okay, it's done. All our info is out there. I ended up asking if we were about to be hit by an alien invasion."

"Did Mr A feed that idea to you?"

"Indirectly. It was a vision he gave me—about building the new world after the so-called 'alien war'."

"Great. You're on safe ground. He should feel he's truly hooked you." He stood up and stretched. "Let's take a little trip while we wait for feedback."

* * *

Gerry, with Jan on the pillion, pulled into a viewpoint parking area amidst rolling wooded hills. The parking area was empty, as it was already late in the afternoon.

They dismounted and looked at the view. Small pastures with grazing sheep and wooded hillsides stretched towards the horizon, where the sun had started to set. Long shadows filled hillside hollows.

"Beautiful, isn't it?" He gestured expansively, like a real estate salesman. "Who needs people when you have this?"

"Are you thinking that in the future this might be off limits to everyone except the elite?"

"It could happen. As I said, future generations might be easier to control than the ones who went through the Sixties and the Thatcher years."

"Meaning these future generations will be happy to take their recreation in government-approved places? Bit like the Third Reich."

"They won't have any desire to challenge official policy. They'll be thoroughly indoctrinated."

"As the poet said: *Bondage with ease than strenuous liberty.*"

"Milton was right. After having been through violent times, people will *want* to do as they're told. They'll believe in the system. They'll believe they helped create it. Dissent will vanish from the planet. And it will disappear because people themselves will be conditioned into reporting and destroying it. The period of adaptation to global warming will be controlled with a relatively small planetary population. The remaining people will lead lives of placid contentment–*comfortably numb*. At least till the next generation realises what has happened." He laughed darkly. "I hope I'm wrong."

His words hit the right notes for her. If there'd been a state-controlled TV in every German living room, Hitler would have won hearts and minds in months. She shuddered to think what could be achieved today by power-obsessed regimes. What *had already* been achieved.

They continued to look at the view as the sun began its final descent below the horizon. Shadows deepened and darkened, and a chilly wind tousled the grasses around the car park.

"It's obviously going to be tough for me to go back to my old life after this, covering county weddings and council meetings."

"D'you think local authorities are exempt from demon infiltration?" he asked with a questioning smile. "All official bodies are centres of influence. They can become foci for political agendas, so why not for demonic ones?"

"I still won't be going back to the paper," she said decisively.

"You're going to lead the Earth First movement. You've been chosen."

"Why shouldn't I be? I've the talent for it. I'll be a modern Joan of Arc!"

"*Jeanne d'Arc* was betrayed by her king. For 'king' read Mr A."

"You're trying to discourage me?"

"Not in the least. Just stating historic facts. Joan may have been schizophrenic. She heard voices that she thought were messages from God."

"Any more comparisons?"

"She was heavily into cross-dressing. Back then it was thought to be a sickness, if not downright heretical."

"I admit I only wear a skirt or a dress to funerals and weddings. You think it would be OTT if I owned a white stallion?"

They laughed, but she felt his mood darken. "While we were out of contact I looked for a convincing military flight path for that light in the field."

"Did you find one?"

"I'm not sure." He shrugged lamely. "I can't honestly say I have for definite."

"It's okay," she said reassuringly, patting his shoulder. "I know where the light was officially heading." She told him her dream, omitting the bit about Hemingway, which she found too distressing to mention.

"An old airstrip with a bunker," he mused aloud. "Perfect. It's not shown on the OS map because it was part of our so-called national security. That's why I couldn't find it."

"But why did the light come down five miles short? Surely Mr A would have had perfect control of his own technology?"

"Because he was targetting you. There's no other explanation. Those two unhappy barmaids were simply unlucky."

She frowned. "Don't you think that's a bit unlikely, that it came down short because of *me*?"

"It worked, didn't it?"

The conversation was cut short as a sedan pulled into the parking area. An elderly couple got out and observed the darkening view.

He studied them with a puckered brow. "We should go. Night's closing in."

"You make night sound like something threatening."

He smiled inscrutably. "It might be."

They climbed onto the Harley and left the parking area.

The elderly couple morphed into multi-eyed demons and stared after them.

* * *

Back at the warehouse Jan and Gerry switched on their laptops and went to the blog to check responses.

"There are hundreds of replies," he exclaimed. "See what I mean? You have a ready-made audience. Now you can start your Earth First movement!"

He sounded so convincing, for a moment she wasn't sure whose side he was on. He must have played similar mind games before, but how would she know? She was a novice.

She ran quickly through the responses. "These are mostly conspiracy guys. They're sceptics. They won't be convinced by my propaganda."

He looked at her darkly. "They're not convinced yet. But we'll see."

"There are guys asking what they can do. How they can help. I'm amazed. Will these people let the authorities sweep the world into a phoney war? ...Not without a massive protest, I'm sure."

"Judging by this they could provide considerable opposition. I'd have thought the spaceship freaks would have outnumbered the conspiracy guys, but it's the other way round. This proves that the most active element out there is firmly into government lies and cover-ups. So Mr A and his human cronies will have their work cut out to get that false-flag alien invasion up and running. This could change your role."

"D'you think I'll still have one?"

"We'll have to assume you will. But we'll need to be more vigilant and cautious. Let's just stay devoted to Mr A and see what happens."

"Shall we reply to these people?"

"We simply haven't time to weed them all out. There could be Special Branch or Black Ops spies among them, but it's impossible to tell which they are."

She recalled the two detectives waiting in the car outside her flat. "These human helpers might be evil, but are they demons?"

He smiled grimly. "That's an open question."

"D'you have a plan?" She suddenly felt dangerously out of her depth.

"It's time for action. We should organise something spectacular and sound a wake-up call. Planet Earth is on the brink of an invasion!"

12

Several hundred protesters had gathered at the field gate behind the Half Moon Inn. Some took photos of the DANGER KEEP OUT sign. A group of protesters were made up like hideously deformed mutants. They unfurled a banner with STOP THE ROT–DEMAND THE TRUTH in bold red letters. Another banner read: SAVE THE PLANET–AN END TO HOMO CORRUPTUS.

The press arrived, including Russell with Alec the photographer. Alec began taking photos, while Russell chatted to protesters and made notes. He spotted Jan and shrugged a silent question, tapping his finger on his notebook. She shook her head.

She had opened a Pandora's box, but had to keep going, had to play the game to its conclusion, whatever the outcome. Standing on an empty beer crate found at the back of the inn, she addressed the excited crowd through a megaphone. Gerry remained anonymous, sitting on the Harley to the side, visor down, looking intimidating all in black on the big bike.

Clearing her throat and taking a deep breath, Jan officially began. "Thanks for coming. If you've read my blog, you'll all know what happened here."

Murmurs of assent floated forward. Some protesters, carrying Geiger counters, started to climb the gate.

"Please don't go into the field," she yelled. "It's dangerous! Radiation levels are high! I can't be responsible if anyone gets hurt!"

Concern rippled through the crowd. The protesters with Geiger counters stepped back.

"We need to know who did this," she continued firmly. "This is *our* country. We need to take it back into *our* protection."

A cheer went up. But Jan, unaware that she was perilously close to crossing a line, simply wondered how much longer she could keep up the double act.

As if in confirmation of her fears, she spotted Ashtar in his familiar flowing robe standing near the inn. She turned away, avoiding any chance of eye contact, waiting for his message. He reappeared at the back of the crowd, staring at her, hindering her capacity to think. No one else, not even Gerry, seemed able to see him and this realization made her feel trapped and vulnerable.

Again she turned, but still he appeared before her. The power of his penetrating gaze began to disorientate her. He seemed to be everywhere and she couldn't avoid him. The reason for her being there became muddled; she struggled to address the protesters and stick to the false-flag script.

"We want to, hmm, provoke a reaction and find out, hmm, who's behind this. ...Is it aliens with new technology? We're owed an explanation." She endeavoured to regain control, but laughed idiotically instead, as if she was drugged. "It could be Humpty Dumpty or the Red Queen. Or the Mad Hatter or the Cheshire Cat."

Ashtar appeared in the field, in the centre of the contaminated area. He stared, his presence confusing her. She felt groggy.

Gerry, realising all was not well, got off the bike and hurried to her side. "What's wrong?"

"He's here. *Everywhere*." Her voice was hoarse and her face displayed intolerable strain.

He looked around. "I don't see him."

"Take my word for it." Her legs felt weak and she leaned on the field gate for support.

"What if no one shows up?" an earnest protester wanted to know.

"If no one comes we'll know they're pretending ignorance," Gerry replied with calm authority. "They won't want to admit the truth!"

"It's aliens," a voice shouted authoritatively from the crowd. "They've taken over my bank!"

Laughter and applause erupted.

"And the government," someone yelled.

"And the media," another voice declared.

"We want democracy," yet another called out. "Accusation without intimidation!"

Jan realised deep in her subconscious mind—a place that had lain dormant for millennia, undisturbed by demons or any imposed authority—that these people were the true future of the planet. They weren't believers in extraterrestrials, but in establishment conspiracies. She tried to speak, but Ashtar had filled her head with what felt like a dense mist that blocked her thoughts.

Deducing her problem, Gerry seized the megaphone and raised his visor. "They'll come," he shouted with authority. "Because the field's radioactive. They can't put us at risk. They're not ready to wipe us out yet."

"They're here," a young woman called out.

Three police vehicles, blue lights flashing, turned off the main road and headed for the field behind the inn. A cheer went up from the massed protesters.

The grim-looking men in the black Mercedes followed the police, but did not get out of their car.

"Be ready for their lies," Gerry bellowed, receiving a roar of approval. "It wasn't a hoax and it wasn't a plane. *This* is the truth–we can see it for ourselves!"

Another cheer went up.

Ashtaroth had abandoned his Ashtar form, appearing directly in front of Jan, feathered like Owlman. She reeled with shock. He attempted to embrace her—or, as she assumed at the time, to smother her. The fleeting touch of feathers induced nausea, disorientation, and terror. Flailing her arms, she tried ineffectually to fend him off.

He pushed her against the field gate. To avoid the touch of his feathers, she had to scramble over it into the field.

"No!" Gerry yelled, realising something horrific was about to happen. The warning made no difference. Jan was trapped in another world with a demon no one could see.

Ashtaroth was before her, his vast wings outspread, radiating a suffocating toxic stench. His pyroclastic breath, hot and corporeal, burned her eyebrows and tufts of hair protruding from the crash helmet. Images of incinerated corpses from the Iraq invasion sprang into her mind—and, horrified, she fled.

Ashtaroth swooped down as she ran along the field, trying to grab her with his razor-sharp talons. As she made what seemed like a futile attempt to escape from him, two figures in protective clothing hurried along the field in pursuit. She reached the place where the light had originally landed as Ashtaroth swooped down again.

She fell on the grass as Ashtaroth hovered over her. She heard his stupendous voice: "Together we could have made a new world. But you betrayed me! You can't deceive me—I can discover *all* secrets!"

He vanished.

Her confusion immediately cleared. She got to her feet and, racing back to the gate, shouted to the gathering. "This is the place. Look at their reaction. Now we know of their guilt! They're going to use this to control us!"

To jeers and mocking applause, the figures in protective clothing grabbed her and led her from the field.

Superintendent Hemingway watched furiously from the edge of the crowd. For a split second she saw him morph into a hideous fur-covered demon. No one else seemed to have noticed.

Jan wrenched herself free. "This is the truth," she cried. "They want to start a war built on lies. Spread the word!"

Uniformed officers, with no identifying insignia, tried to grab her, but she evaded them, darting into the crowd which linked arms to protect her.

Suddenly Gerry was there on the Harley. "Let's go!" he yelled. She leaped on the pillion and they sped away to more cheers and applause.

* * *

Gerry gunned the Harley down the main road with the black Mercedes pursuing close behind. It was impossible for them to escape on main roads and motorways, even at 125 mph. As soon as he could he turned off into a warren of country lanes. He knew the area, but his choice of route was limited as he had to cross a river before he'd be able to shake off their pursuers.

The nearest bridge over the river was five miles away. As he pulled ahead of the Mercedes, he was grateful for the many hours he'd spent on the Pembrey bike-racing circuit. Those hours might save their lives.

With the Mercedes three hundred yards behind, he thundered across the bridge at 90 mph. As soon as they entered open country on the other side, the passenger in the pursuing vehicle opened fire. Bullets flew past the speeding Harley. Gerry leaned the bike into a tight curve and headed into woodland on a narrow dirt track. The Mercedes couldn't follow and abandoned the chase.

Five minutes later he eased the bike into the back of a small horse trailer, which was hitched to Jan's BMW hidden among the trees. Exchanging biking leathers for casual gear, the two leaped into the car with Gerry behind the wheel. They followed a bridleway and headed for the nearest motorway.

"They actually shot at us," she exclaimed, still stunned.

"I didn't think they would dare. Just shows how much is at stake for them."

"Can we risk going back online?" she asked.

"I don't think so. But I've a good friend who might be willing to take over the blog till he's sussed and has to shut down."

"What about us? We'll have to vanish for a while, won't we?"

His expression grim, he nodded emphatically. "Either that ... or *be disappeared*."

Suddenly from nowhere, Ashtaroth in Owlman form appeared in front of them. He swooped down at the car, as if intent on embracing it and blotting out their visibility. Jan shrieked in helpless terror. Gerry had to make an instant choice: brake or accelerate. He chose the latter. If he braked, the trailer could swing and drag them off the narrow country road.

Time of the Demon

Just as it seemed a collision was inevitable, Ashtaroth vanished and a blinding red-and-white revolving light shot skywards at tremendous speed.

Gerry slowed the car, but didn't stop. "Let's hope he doesn't pull that stunt on the motorway–might be a bit awkward trying to explain how we caused a multiple pile-up!"

She admired his nerve. She knew she'd have braked, skidded, lost control, and probably killed them both. Then she noticed sweat streaming down his face.

"I didn't have time to be afraid," he said softly, glancing at her. "The sweat is the after-effect, when adrenalin's kicked in. In a few minutes, it'll pass and I'll feel cold."

How many times had he faced a life-and-death situation, she wondered. He seemed familiar with the pattern. "Mr A knows you're with me now, doesn't he?"

"Maybe he's known all along, which makes me think he has another agenda."

"What? No secret weapons after all?"

"The Half Moon thing might be a distraction to keep the conspiracy guys busy."

"What about my vision and the Earth First movement?" she asked, puzzled. "Is all that over?"

"It might have been a dry run, to test the degree of wised-up opposition."

"But Mr A would already be aware of that if he knows all the world's secrets," she objected. "Why bother to go to such lengths with lights and choppers?"

"Perhaps to convince his neoliberal cronies that a different approach might be needed."

"No phoney war? No false flags?"

"I don't know. There are countless ways for Mr A to make moves. We'll just have to be ready for them."

13

When they reached the warehouse on the industrial estate, Gerry got busy on his laptop in the office while Jan drank coffee as she studied her notebook. He talked as he worked. "As agreed, I've lifted your Half Moon piece and sent it off to TRUFON. It's in your name. If they offer the media a few choice paragraphs, you want a cut of any proceeds. I'll be keeping in touch with them. I think once TRUFON has done some front-running, you could tempt a publishing house with the offer of a book. TRUFON will want a sizeable cut as your agents. But they have the clout to push the deal through. I'll help you with any editing work they insist on."

"But we haven't bottomed out on this," she objected. "We still don't know for definite who's involved, at what level in the military establishment, and how extensive their global connections might be. I can't believe Mr A didn't know the conspiracy guys were going to be out in force. I mean, these are the guys who won't buy the attack-from-outer-space scenario. I can't see the point of a dry run when the outcome's so clear. And I can't understand why I had to be involved."

"The incident at the inn was a perfect preparation. It fulfilled its purpose."

She eyed him blankly. "I don't follow you."

"In our speculative situation Mr A's military cronies have to convince the most hardened sceptics that an alien invasion is for real. If our small protest was even fifty per cent conspiracy guys, the Black Ops people would know they've a major propaganda issue to deal with. And so, with Mr A's help, the conspiracy guys might find themselves marginalised, especially if a more potent version of the white light was used to wipe out an entire city, maybe somewhere in the Middle East–Tehran, for instance. Or further east, possibly Pyongyang."

"I got the impression Mr A was giving up," she told him. "He'd said 'together we could have made a new world'—past tense. And I also had the distinct feeling when he flew at the car that it was a valediction of some sort." She shrugged. "He saw the strength of the opposition and called it a day."

"Don't you think that was what he *wanted* you to believe?"

She was annoyed with herself. Of course it was. "You could be right."

"He'll never give up. Demons don't do defeat. Unless they make war on each other."

"So what exactly is going on? I'm getting confused."

Crossing hands across his broad chest, Greg leaned back in the chair. "I think what happened this morning was the start of something more sinister than we realise. In itself it might have been a distraction. While we're putting all our attention on the Half Moon thing, we're not looking for other stuff."

She frowned. "What *other stuff*?"

"I don't know, because we're not looking." He offered a dry, fleeting smile. "I think your book has to reflect that. It has to go deeper, prepare its readers for anything from a Half Moon type of weapon, to a false messianic resurgence, even a lethal virus outbreak. And, while all this distraction is going on, a massive demonic infiltration transpires ... unnoticed."

"You're frightening me."

"I just think we should be more cautious. Seems to me that elements within certain western national security services have done a fiendish deal with Mr A's legions to create RFOs ... to spread death on a highly selective basis. A devilishly clever way to get rid of any rogue element with nuclear capability that threatens western aims."

"What the hell are RFOs?"

"Radioactive Flying Objects–what else? Don't you see– they can claim to be fighting for human freedom?

"You're right," she agreed quietly, perturbed. "I can understand that."

"Add a religious element to the mix and who knows where it could go? The key human players would believe that a one-world government was within their grasp. The United States, Russia, and China control everything. Or maybe just the US. But they could be mistaken. With global warming the whole thing could fragment into city states and ethnic enclaves fighting each other, like in medieval times. Mr A would *really* enjoy that."

"How can humans make deals with demons? It's not going to work, is it?"

"I'm glad you see that. Once demons are involved, you won't get rid of them easily. And their agenda will be beyond their human cronies' grasp."

"So we're looking for something more subtle than RFOs, which could just be a distraction?" she reasoned.

"It could be happening already. We don't know yet what we're looking for."

She coughed and he looked at her, alarmed. "How are you feeling?"

Jan fingered her neck and shrugged. "I'm okay. It's only a bit of a cold."

He eyed her searchingly. "You'll tell me if you feel worse?"

"Of course. Don't worry." A thought struck her. "Even sensational news can get deliberately swamped and sidelined. We mustn't let that happen. Maybe we could run the story initially as a series of instalments in TRUFON's mag, adding more revelations as we discover them. Then do the book afterwards."

"That's a great idea. I'll get on to TRUFON about it."

Time of the Demon

"I've lots of pics we can use—the inn surrounded by police tape and the field itself. Shame that I didn't get one of Hemingway."

"Can you photograph a demon?" he asked doubtfully. "I confess I've never tried. I can imagine the camera bursting into flames."

They laughed. Her laughter ended in a prolonged coughing fit. After pressing a handkerchief to her mouth, she found it covered in blood.

He was on his feet in a moment, staring at her in dismay. "Jan—you're ill!" Hurriedly, he grabbed a heavy blanket from a bin in a corner. As he covered her, she finally told him about the dream, where Hemingway held the sphere of light with her trapped inside.

"I'm sorry I didn't mention it before, but I couldn't. I see now that it was prophetic."

"You're suggesting all that's happened so far was *inevitable*?"

Tears rolled down her cheeks. "How can we beat these demons when they have such great power? It seems we're no more than puppets."

"Leave demons for now," he said sternly. "You're coming with me."

She looked at him in alarm. "Where are we going?"

"In an ideal world, I'd take you to a specialist private hospital. But that would ring all the wrong alarm bells. You'd end up with Jess and Gina. Or worse."

"But if you think it's that serious, isn't it worth the risk? It would be great publicity for the book."

"At what price? You could die—or simply disappear. That wouldn't be helpful at all, to you or the book."

"I'd be too well known. I'd be untouchable."

"You'd vanish, believe me. If you had to appear in public, they'd find an actress lookalike. It's been done before, remember? And they'd use the opportunity to discredit the book. Make you look inept and uncritical, easily led by the conspiracy movement. Your name and the book would be forgotten, except by a few die-hard extremists."

"What's the alternative?"

"I'm taking you to a friend's place." As he spoke, he keyed a number into his mobile. "We should go. It's a long drive."

"Photograph me," she said earnestly. "Make a record of this. If I'm as ill as you think I am, it's crucial stuff for the book."

He appeared as if he might refuse. "It would only prove useful when we have objective third-party corroboration."

"We'll get that. Photograph me," she insisted. "Just do it."

His call was answered and he nodded reluctant assent.

* * *

They sped down the motorway in Jan's BMW with Gerry once again at the wheel. Before they left the industrial estate he destroyed the surveillance evidence of their arrival at the warehouse. Sure police nationwide would be looking for her vehicle, he put false plates on it.

She looked pale. Blood flecked her lower lip and chin.

"Okay there?"

"Yes. Thanks." Her voice sounded weak and she seemed confused. "Where are we going? Not to a hospital?"

"We've been through that. I'd never see you again."

"D'you want to see me again?"

"You know I do."

"So where are you taking me?" Her eyes were filled with sudden anxiety.

"We're going to see the good guys. The only people I can trust. And it's a different kind of magic altogether, nothing to do with ufology. I've come to the conclusion there are no good guys in that world at all." He changed motorways, heading west.

"You're lucky to have such friends. I'd be lost without you." Her voice was so faint he could hardly hear her words.

"Well, I'm here now. And I intend to look after you."

She coughed more blood.

"Don't talk," he advised. "We'll be there in an hour." He knew the damage from the demon's actions might be impossible to heal, but he'd witnessed several healings the rational world would have called miracles, so he had faith in his friends and their otherworld contacts.

Half an hour later he turned off the motorway. After another half hour he was threading his way through a network of country lanes. Ahead were the November skeletons of ancient indigenous woodland and on the southern horizon the long murky outline of high moors.

* * *

She'd fallen asleep. Gerry pulled up in a lay-by and lifted her onto the back seat, making her as comfortable as he could. She wasn't aware of the last stage of the journey, with him winding deeper into a wild and rugged landscape. Eventually he turned on to a private road and followed it for a mile through hills dotted with ancient oak, holly and hawthorn.

A row of tidy old-fashioned cottages appeared against a backdrop of dense woodland. He pulled up to the door of the first cottage.

Two muscular young men, dark-haired and wind-tanned, stepped from the well-tended cottage. They greeted Gerry like an old friend and lifted Jan gently from the car. They placed her on a stretcher, then took her inside. Gerry followed, carrying their few possessions in a travel bag.

The men took the unconscious Jan into a back parlour where a peat fire burned in an old iron stove. After laying her on a simple divan, several young women appeared and seated themselves alongside, laying their hands on Jan's body. A striking woman of thirty-five, tall and raven haired, dressed in the robes of a coven priestess, entered silently. She and Gerry exchanged warm smiles. "Thanks for agreeing to this, Morwenna," he said quietly. "It's in all our interests that my friend Jan survives."

"How could we do otherwise?" Morwenna gestured to the women who surrounded Jan. "They're giving her a charge of life energy, so she has strength to get through what will follow."

"She was exposed to a massive dose of radioactivity. Will a healing really be possible?" His face revealed both hope and doubt.

"I won't be healing her," Morwenna replied matter-of-factly. "Her cure, if there is one, will be performed by others, for whom I cannot speak." She embraced him in a gesture of sympathy, then went to the divan and placed a slender hand on Jan's forehead. "She's very cold. We'll take her now." She addressed the young women. "Get her ready." She turned to Gerry. "Do you love her, Gawen?"

"She knows me as Gerry." He smiled sadly at the unconscious figure of Jan. "If you'd asked me that a week ago, I'd have said I wasn't sure," he replied solemnly. "But now I have no doubt that I do."

"She has youth and your love on her side. Are you prepared to help?"

He bowed his head. "I am."

The young women gently raised Jan into a seated position so Morwenna could fasten a warm shawl about her shoulders.

"We must go," Morwenna announced. She took Jan's hands in hers. "It's only a ten-minute walk and a whole otherworld away."

"Are you going across the water?"

"We've no choice. There can't be a healing for her anywhere else."

14

The path led down a gentle slope through mixed deciduous woodland. The two men had been joined by two others, equally muscular and young; all four were now dressed in loose coven robes. Jan lay on the stretcher. Gerry, Morwenna and the women, the latter also in coven robes, followed.

Ahead was a small picturesque lake surrounded by tall trees. The lake rippled as a light breath of wind danced across it. Treetops swayed and branches creaked like primal voices.

The foursome placed the stretcher on a prepared wooden rest. Jan appeared still to be unconscious. Gerry watched her with deep concern as Morwenna and the young women cast off their clothes. Naked, they began to project a very simple sound, a rising and falling cadence.

Ripples on the lake grew still and the water's surface became as smooth as a mirror. Daylight slowly faded. The trees stood motionless, like intricate carvings in the windless air.

Morwenna and the women stopped singing as a patch of mist, like a little cloud, rose from the water. The mist grew denser, a pale amber light glowing at its centre.

Morwenna glanced at Gerry. Also naked, he lifted Jan from the stretcher and slowly walked into the lake towards the light. The mist enveloped them and gradually they began to fade from sight.

The women watched from the bank and began singing again. The four men, now naked, joined them; their voices swelling into a deep drone. As the drone reverberated through the woodland, Gerry and Jan appeared to merge with the light in the mist.

"We must leave them," Morwenna instructed. "Her fate is now in the hands of the earth spirits."

* * *

As Jan slept, fragments of dreams, or possibly memories, came and went. She was unable to do more than observe the dream moments coming and going, like the flickering images of an old film. Then the fragments ceased and a longer sequence began.

She was flying over the earth in what seemed like an OOBE. Dead bodies lay everywhere, in city streets and open spaces, in fields and in the hills, floating in lakes and in the sea. With a rising sense of horror she realised that she–or a power-hungry alter ego–was responsible for the carnage. The announcement of a Great Awakening had come from her. Or, rather, from the toga-clad Ashtar through her. She had been his willing mouthpiece, believing that together they would create a beautiful new world. She had been intoxicated by the adulation her followers lavished on her.

Then the killing started, with entire cultures wiped out. Genocide after genocide. The survivors, led by a pseudo-religious group called The Reborn, were pleased with the success of The Rebirth as it was labelled. The Reborn were everywhere, in the walled and heavily-weaponised communities they set up in the former temperate, more habitable latitudes. The dead were an irrelevance. The only people who would mourn them were already dead themselves.

At first she thought The Reborn were humans. But she came to realise they were minor-order demons who had infiltrated the human world during the chaos brought about by global warming and the belated, mostly ineffective measures governments introduced to combat climate change.

The Rebirth had been preceded by a virus spread by UFOs. Military response to the so-called alien attacks had been uncoordinated and futile, as alien spacecraft dematerialised when attacked. The clean-up was supposed to last a few months, but the process of decontamination stalled. No one (except Ashtar, she realised) had foreseen that rats would become immune to the virus. As the rats devoured the corpses, their fleas spread a horrific plague, like a modern-day Black Death. Sixty per cent of the world's population died from it and from various territorial wars against The Reborn.

Ashtar and his group of higher-order demonic accomplices departed the plague-ridden earth in a stupendous display of revolving lights. She remained behind, abandoned and powerless, to be denounced by The Reborn, tied to a stake in a field of rotting corpses, waiting for the fleas to infect her and the rats to eat her alive.

Before the carnage began an attempt was made to turn The Rebirth into a full-blown religious crusade. The Risen Christ appeared in sub-Saharan Africa and formed a parallel, more mystical movement than the austere and repressive Reborn. The crusade's mission was to annihilate all other religions by example or, if necessary, by force. As the death toll rose from the plague, the Christ figure abruptly disappeared. "Second Thoughts on a Second Coming?" was the headline question around the world.

The Risen Christ was claimed to be the illegitimate offspring of an ousted African dictator, a revelation quickly denounced as fake news by his more dedicated followers. Astonished eye witnesses said he boarded his 'strangely-shaped' private plane and vanished before matters got entirely out of hand, and he became a scapegoat for the escalating horror and was crucified, according to precedent. No one saw The Risen Christ again.

She was now the sole target for the wrath of The Reborn. She had tried to blame the entire debacle on someone called Ashtar, or Ashok, but no persons with those names were found to exist. She had muttered incoherently about being misled by demons, that the tragedy had been a diabolical trick, and these demons were feasting off the horror and fear. This, however, was attributed by The Reborn to the ravings of an unhinged mind.

Her name could no longer be spoken. Guardians of the Community had powers to arrest anyone who mentioned her. The years of plague gradually began to fade. Climate change was irreversible, but the heavily-armed communities of survivors adapted to the extreme environment, using slaves to carry out the more dangerous tasks that required excursions beyond the enclaves' walls.

The Reborn employed scholars to create an account of history, in which it was claimed that the world had been saved by the Power of Love. The few misguided enough to question this version were denounced as subversives and disappeared.

The Reborn set up a School of Love where students were systematically indoctrinated with 'the truth'. After graduation they lived passive lives of contented docility working for The Reborn, who the deranged sociopath Jan Barnes accused of being demons.

* * *

Jan had the impression that this OOBE, or vision, belonged to a potential parallel life, which had been prevented from becoming reality due to the hectic events of the protest at the Half Moon Inn and its aftermath. It was a warning vision of the direction events might have taken. This, she realised, was Ashtaroth's real agenda, but she was free from him now and from the distractions of RFOs, viruses and crusades. She was free simply to live or to die.

After the OOBE she slept more deeply. At first she was aware of nothing at all. Then, slowly, new images began to appear, initially more like shadows than definite forms. Gradually the shadows faded, or merged, into the walls of a room, or perhaps a cave.

All sense of time disappeared. How long she lay in the cave-like place was impossible to tell. It could have been days, or even years. Time was of a completely different nature and so difficult to comprehend it was as though it didn't exist at all.

The waiting seemed inevitable and natural, as if it was a stage she had to go through before she could move on to the next phase of her life–or death. Just when it seemed she would be there for ever, Jan felt herself lifted as if by an updraft of air. She rose on it for what appeared to be only a few moments. Then she stopped and became motionless once more.

There was no tunnel, no emergence into a world of light. She wasn't having a conventional post-mortem experience. There was a definite environment, a context, but was it physical? The idea of being in a cave became stronger and more plausible. At first, the cave was almost entirely dark and empty. But then she felt hands pulling her violently in many directions. She wanted to protest, but the faculty of speech had abandoned her.

The pulling continued, and she accepted this might be the only remaining reality. It was painful, but she had no choice other than surrender to the experience of being torn into tiny pieces and gradually being made whole again.

With an overwhelming sense of relief she realised the pulling had stopped and she was moving again. Hands were lifting her, carrying her on what seemed like a cool and pleasant journey. The light increased, but her eyes were covered and she was unable to see.

An odd sound frightened her because of its strangeness. She wanted to blot out the sound, but had no means to do this. Then she realised it was familiar— a human voice.

The voice was saying something she couldn't make out. Then it became clear. "We have removed the bandage. You can open your eyes."

She had no idea where she was. In spite of feeling displaced she found she could open her eyes and she peered at a world of flickering shadows. They seemed benign and warm and she felt safe. Overwhelmed by colossal fatigue she shut her eyes again and slept.

* * *

Gerry and Jan sat in a cosy parlour by a glowing stove. He noticed that she seemed to have made a complete recovery; her eyes were clear, her demeanour composed.

"So you're really Gawen?" She looked at him with good-humoured disbelief. "Is that your birth name, or another alias?"

"It's my birth name. I'm a Cornishman. I prefer to keep that name secret and borrow other people's when I'm on the wrong side of the River Tamar. We can stick with Gerry if you like." He laughed. "It's the name that embodies most of the history that has led us to where we are now."

"Are you a member of Morwenna's coven?"

"I'm not the sort of person to join anything, no matter how worthy or enlightened it may be. I prefer to be a free agent, as I once said, responsible for my own actions. That way, if I fall foul of the authorities, I'll leave no trail that could implicate others."

They had not talked about her healing. She had no idea to what extent he'd been involved and preferred not to ask. That the healing appeared successful satisfied her for the time being. She had left this world and entered one of the many otherworlds that she now found easier to accept: a benign otherworld of peace and transformation.

When she had regained consciousness she found she had been 'away' for a month. A lot had happened during that time and she was keen to catch up.

Gerry was happy to oblige. "The authorities are calling the incident at the inn a 'toxic spill'. Like it was some kind of agro-chemical accident. No mention of a UFO. Seems they can only manage one area of denial at a time. Of course, the conspiracy guys aren't buying it."

"What about the blog?"

"I can see your memory's returned to full health." He winked and grinned. "The blog's thriving. It's now a website called s-p-i.com, or Strange Phenomena Investigations. I'm partly responsible for managing it. It's globally active, with witnesses to weird events reporting almost daily. There's even a secret network of supporters prepared to hide vulnerable witnesses from the authorities. Absolutely no one's having anything to do with the establishment's lies."

"How can you protect the site from establishment infiltration and," she faltered, "from demons?"

"At first glance it's a very boring site, with lots of banal chatter. But there are coded links to other sites where the real discussions happen."

"It's not exclusively a conspiracy site?"

"Not on the surface. We've had fascinating reports on lake monster sightings in Russia, so-called alien animals in Scandinavia, and ghostly happenings around the construction of a new bypass in the east of England."

"I might have a piece to post. It's a fable about the downfall of a gullible female who was tricked by a demon. It's timeless. It could go back into the ages of the first civilisations. I saw it all in a visionary dream."

She shared a little of the sequence of events in her OOBE. He listened without interruption.

"I got to experience something truly chilling: the depth of indulgence of a demon watching destruction, the horrific pleasure of a demon feeding off blood and sickness and terror. It was an appalling revelation."

He was silent for a while, thinking over her account. "Seems the only winners as usual are Mr A and his legions, except perhaps for what you've called The Reborn. Have you any idea who they could be?"

She shook her head. "It wasn't clear. They seemed to be a mysterious sect that emerged at some point in the chaos and took over."

"What's your intuition tell you?"

"It told me, in the OOBE, they were demons. Now ... I'm not so sure."

"They weren't human puppets?"

"It's hard to tell now I'm back in ordinary consciousness. Demons in human form look like humans. Unless you invent some kind of hi-tech demon detector, you don't know which is which. A rogue element in the military and among Black Ops guys could all be demons or humans, or a mixture of both. You can't tell. In my vision, The Reborn seemed to appear from nowhere. My alter ego had no hesitation in denouncing them as demons. If I could contact my other self at will I may be able to see through a demon's human disguise."

"You should cultivate that connection. It could prove a tremendous asset."

"I can try. But it might involve me in a life I don't feel strong enough yet to survive."

They were silent again, deep in thought.

He put more fuel in the stove. "The world's population was halved in your vision?"

"At least."

"One of the Georgia Guidestones' ideals realised."

She nodded in agreement. "But don't the demons need us?"

"They do. They can't wipe us out. What sport would be left for them apart from fighting each other?"

He paused to think. "Whether it's from RFOs, viruses or whatever, The Reborn seem to have been left in control, like a super elite, am I right?"

"That's what I felt. But it could be misinformation. It's hard to tell fact from fiction in Mr A's world."

"Let's assume it's fact and these are the guys Mr A puts in charge. Humans or demons, they'll be subject to his will, but they may not know who's controlling them. It's hard to imagine humans being so thoroughly brainwashed, so my money's on The Reborn as demons." He uttered a brief self-deprecating laugh. "But I have lost bets before."

"You're thinking The Reborn will farm us directly, like battery hens, these so-called graduates of the School of Love?"

"They'll create arenas for blood sports to keep the graduates distracted. Mr A is obviously impressed by Roman urban life. They may give away free bread, if the climate allows them to grow cereals. We've already paved the way with survival-of-the-fittest TV shows. Then they'll probably get bored and instigate a violent revolution against themselves, which they'll suppress with massive loss of life. It will serve two purposes: population control and first-order entertainment for demons. Then more control, more sport, another revolution. Around and around."

"Why not leave the world as it is? There's enough war and terror already. There'll be huge fires and floods due to out-of-control climate change. Surely that's enough fun for any number of demonic legions?"

"That's an interesting thought. But demons are meddlers, always stirring the human stew. As for climate change, you have to ask who's ultimately responsible. Can humans really be so reckless? If they can, it's a terrible indictment."

"We need a new plan." Jan's manner took on great urgency. "Something on a massive scale to drive that demon away from our reality."

"I've been working on that," he replied with a fleeting smile.

Morwenna entered, dressed in outdoors' gear. "Everyone's in," she stated matter-of-factly. "I've had the last confirmations today. We just need to know when."

"Are you up for more danger?" Gerry asked Jan.

"It might depend on what kind."

"We'll merely be spectators this time. I hope there'll be minimal risk."

"I'm in. It sounds intriguing."

He turned to Morwenna. "Midwinter celebrations are approaching. The psychic energy circuit will become more highly charged. Can we do it this next weekend?"

15

Gerry and Jan headed for an old tin-mining area in the nearby hills, where sightings of Owlman had occurred during the summer.

"You're officially a missing person," he said. "Does that bother you?"

"Not in the least," she replied with a smile. "I don't want to be found."

"The world of aliases can be tricky to navigate," he grinned.

She laughed. "I'd be happy to give it a whirl!"

They parked the 4x4 away from the eyes of passing motorists. Light was becoming grainy with the approaching dusk. The apprehension Jan had felt since they left Morwenna's sanctuary began to ebb. It was time for action and steady nerves. She was looking forward to it.

He passed her a bottle of herbal mixture and she took a small sip.

"I'm half way out of this world most of the time now." She passed the bottle back. "I think it's the result of the healing."

"You're on your way to becoming a shaman." He drank half of the mixture. "I need to play catch-up!"

They followed a rough path that led through a wild rocky landscape. There was no sound. The bushes were motionless. The scene was illuminated by a sourceless hazy glow. They had crossed the invisible threshold where otherworlds began.

The old mine workings appeared; the derelict remains of long-abandoned buildings loomed through the haze. Gerry indicated an area of large grass-covered boulders, and they went over to sit and wait.

"Let's hope everyone's ready," she telepathised.

"And Mr A's at home," he replied gravely, "*not* expecting to be tricked!"

"You think he might not appear? That he might have read our minds?"

"I'm hoping his arrogance will overcome his caution."

* * *

The old Celtic covens of the western counties assembled at their traditional sites to observe the midwinter sunset. As the sun disappeared below the horizon, fires sprang into vivid life. Silhouettes, with arms raised to the night sky, invoked the old magic. A throbbing chant, expanding into a flowing ocean of power, filled the air. Several generations had passed since such a massive force of energy had been raised. The chant continued to build until a Cone of Power took form. The energy held steady, awaiting direction.

In the old tin mine the derelict buildings hovered mysteriously at the edge of a newly risen mist. Gerry and Jan waited patiently. The silence deepened. The air itself seemed filled with oppressive pressure, as if a massive ticking bomb lay hidden nearby.

Ashtar appeared in his flowing robes. Jan and Gerry turned away, avoiding a head-on confrontation. "You have come to try to destroy me," the demon said sternly. "But your efforts are futile. How can you harm me when I am more powerful than any god that has ever existed?"

He reproduced into a hundred identical images of himself. Their combined voices reverberated around the old mine buildings. "I am *everywhere*. Before time was, I am and always will be. The new world will be mine and your efforts are nothing!" The multiple images vanished.

The mist slowly thinned and the night sky became visible, packed with glittering stars that seemed to sizzle. Ashtar reappeared and morphed into his archetypal form: a demon more terrifying than Owlman, with gigantic feathered wings and the massive head of a hideous fanged monster. His mouth belched flame and long, needle-sharp fangs dripped blood.

An overpowering stench of rotting corpses filled the air. Gerry and Jan struggled to breathe. With a stupendous roar, Ashtaroth sprang towards Jan, who stood her ground.

Gerry and Jan cried with one voice, "Release the Power!"

He pulled her behind the protection of a large boulder as a massive bolt of blinding lightning struck Ashtaroth. Giant silhouettes, visible in the brilliant light, poured from the underworld.

"See!" Gerry called out. "King Arthur and the Wild Hunt ride tonight!"

Gigantic armour-clad riders on towering battle steeds as tall as oak trees surged like a colossal tidal wave towards them. Lightning bolts flared around the riders, and their energy flashed from the war band's raised swords.

Ashtaroth burst into flames. The hidden demons in the old mine erupted from their lairs, screaming in agony as they were cut down by the lightning-charged weapons. Emitting a raucous cry of rage, Ashtaroth attempted to escape the Wild Hunt by morphing into a spinning blue-and-yellow light. But before the light could assume its full form, it exploded. He transformed into a small red-and-white disc and shot away at tremendous speed into the night sky.

* * *

Hemingway, dressed as a senior military officer, sat at the head of a large boardroom table, surrounded by similarly attired cronies. As one, they morphed into demons and burst into flames. Some jumped from windows and fell screaming into the streets below. Others seized human colleagues and destroyed them in an orgy of annihilation.

Demons across the west of England burst into flames: in cars, in offices, in the streets. They hurled themselves from roofs, under buses, into rivers. The human population fled in terror and shut themselves away in their houses, in churches, community centres and village halls. Some prayed. Others wept. Most simply stared at one another in stunned silence.

* * *

The old mine workings were a scene of smouldering desolation. There was no sign of Ashtaroth or his demons, merely heaps of ashes and spitting embers.

Overwhelmed, Gerry and Jan embraced.

"I thought the Wild Hunt was just a story," she said. "A means of keeping children away from the woods at night when wolves prowled the landscape."

He laughed. "I suppose it would have done that too. We had to open a portal into the world of the dead. Samhain would have been the best time, but it seems midwinter worked quite well. Only King Arthur and the sacred dead have the power to defeat a demon like Ashtaroth. They've joined us in this war. They've given us permission to commit acts of spontaneous violence that can't be read by demons in advance."

"But it's not over," she said solemnly.

"No, it's not. But at least we've proved that all the region's traditional pagan groups can come together for the common good and work the old magic."

They left the mine and returned to her car. A waxing moon played hide and seek among clusters of altocumulus and the night wind stirred the trees into slow shamanic dancers. They could see lights of vehicles in the distance. The world of demons and the Wild Hunt had silently faded.

They drove out of the upland country. By the time they reached lower ground the first spark of the midwinter sunrise was showing above the horizon. An entire night had passed in what seemed a mere couple of hours.

"We've a book to write," she declared. "We can do it now we have something that looks like an ending, even if it might only be provisional."

"I think I might have a publisher interested. They want to read the first fifty pages. If they like what they see, we might get a deal. It'll help spread awareness. But first, I think we should rest and relax a while."

She kissed his cheek. "Now that sounds promising." An unwelcome thought crossed her mind. "But we'll still have to be on our guard. Those Black Ops guys will never stop looking for us, will they?"

"Not if they think we pose some kind of threat."

"Then there's Mr A. D'you think the lightning strike was seriously wounding?"

"Doubtful. He's been around for millennia and no one's been able to finish him off. I'm sure he'll be back before long with another rigged deck of old tricks."

"Demons are already among us. They're determined to copy the human blueprint. We're going to have a battle some time soon, otherwise they'll swamp us."

"Demons have limited imagination. They might be tricky and devious, but we can outwit them. Trap them. Destroy them. There's just one big problem."

Jan nodded and sighed. "The higher-order demons can read our minds."

"Exactly. They see us coming."

"How d'you tell the difference between an emotionally repressed human and a demon with retarded feelings?"

"You can't, unless you test them," he explained solemnly. "If a demon moves in next door, you won't find him owning any pets, unless it's a parrot or goldfish he gets just for show. And they won't last long in such poisonous company. Cats are pretty psychic. Their reaction to the presence of demons is extreme. Dogs aren't as good, but they react. Just see if your demon neighbour will stroke your dog. He won't even try, because he knows the dog will bark and back away in fear, or fix him with a lethal snarl. So there are simple ways demons can be identified."

"Then what? You can't shoot them!"

He chuckled. "You place a secret sigil close by and summon the Wild Hunt."

"Just like that?"

"You see the scale of the task. But we must make a start."

"We should become anonymous hunters. Faceless assassins."

"You've got the idea."

Gerry pulled into a field gateway, got out and unlocked the gate, then drove down a track to a small woodside cottage surrounded with apple trees.

"This is mine when I need it," was all he offered in explanation. "There's the ghost of an old beekeeper out back who keeps an eye on the hives for me. I've learned a lot about bees from that very wise gentleman."

She looked at him in astonishment, not knowing if he was serious. He laughed at her confusion and parked the car round the side of the cottage so it was hidden from the track. She caught a glimpse of beehives among the fruit trees.

"Our rest time starts now," he said. "Let's make the most of it. The bees will tell us if there are dubious characters about. They can smell demons a mile away. And there's a pair of ravens in residence in the wood beyond the orchard. You can tell by their calls if something's amiss."

"The birds and the bees?" She laughed.

"The bringers of wisdom." He unlocked the cottage door. "Our protectors."

"Well," she said, "we've reached the end of one road."

"And the beginning of another."

DEAR READER

Dear reader,

We hope you enjoyed reading *Time of the Demon*. Please take a moment to leave a review, even if it's a short one. Your opinion is important to us.

Discover more books by authors Ian Taylor at

https://www.nextchapter.pub/authors/ian-taylor

Want to know when one of our books is free or discounted? Join the newsletter at

http://eepurl.com/bqqB3H

Best regards,

Ian Taylor and the Next Chapter Team

You might also like:

Catching Phantoms by Ian and Rosi Taylor

To read the first chapter for free go to:
https://www.nextchapter.pub/books/catching-phantoms

Time Of The Demon
ISBN: 978-4-86750-693-6
Mass Market

Published by
Next Chapter
1-60-20 Minami-Otsuka
170-0005 Toshima-Ku, Tokyo
+818035793528

8th June 2021

www.ingramcontent.com/pod-product-compliance
Lightning Source LLC
LaVergne TN
LVHW032010070526
838202LV00059B/6373